BURDEN OF GUILT

PAUL J. TEAGUE

This is a work of fiction. Names, characters, businesses, places, events and incidents are either the products of the author's imagination or used in a fictitious manner. Any resemblance to actual persons, living or dead, or actual events is purely coincidental.

This book was inspired by a love of Fort William, Spean Bridge, Glenfinnan, Mallaig, Inverness ... in fact the entire area.

I visited as a child, returned on honeymoon and keep coming back.

If you ever travel to the area, please support the communities and businesses that are mentioned in this book with some enthusiastic tourist spending.

PROLOGUE

July 1999 Katy watched as her boyfriend burned, unable to escape from the wooden structure as it was engulfed in flames. The fire was ferocious in the wind, with huge flares sweeping across the garden, keeping the huddle of horrified onlookers at bay. The air was filled with the crackle of burning wood and the sobbing of the five friends, distraught at the thought of Elijah trapped inside.

Driven back by the searing heat, they watched in terror, unable to think of any action that they could take to extinguish the inferno. They were forced to sit it out and wait until the horror ended. They were miles from anywhere. Elijah didn't stand a chance. There was nothing to stop the flames once they'd started, and they consumed the building in less than half an hour.

There were no phone boxes nearby. The cabin was nestled at the foot of a hill, surrounded by trees, and at the end of a long, winding track. Even if help could have been summoned, it would have been too late. They were too far away from the nearest town.

It had seemed like such a good idea: two weeks in the

Scottish Highlands, a log cabin in the middle of nowhere, and a car boot filled with booze. They'd finished their year one exams, they had a long summer ahead of them, and they were in love – young, idealistic love, their whole lives yet to live. They had nearly four months away from university and nothing to do with all that time.

Five of them had piled into the car – it was a wonder there was any room for the clothes and toiletries. They didn't care, all they could think of was two weeks of sleeping in, laughter and drinking. But it all turned to shit fast. The easy-come, easy-go bubble of university life had quickly evaporated as the reality of living in a cabin with an erratic boiler and night-time visits from the local vermin had set in. The laughter turned to bitching, the booze remained unopened in the fridge, and relationships became tense. What had seemed like too short a time to go on holiday soon turned into an eternity. Two weeks became a lifetime and plans to share a student house in the new term began to look hasty and ill-conceived.

But it never should have come to this. They watched and wept as the wooden structure was transformed into a smoking, charred ruin. Elijah was in there somewhere. There would be nothing left of him. The squabbles seemed so petty now. How had they let it get so out of hand?

Eventually, in the darkness of the night time, the emergency services arrived, alerted by a farmer from across the valley. They'd thought it was a woodland fire started by careless campers. It turned out to be much worse. When the police arrived, they found five shocked friends standing and watching the scene before them, stunned at what had happened. It would take them a long time to recover from what they'd seen.

But, in spite of the tears, was Elijah's death really the

freak accident the Sheriff recorded it as? Nobody could understand why he hadn't got out well before the flames took hold. Perhaps there was a reason why he hadn't escaped. The repercussions of that day would be felt for many years to come.

CHAPTER ONE

Katy woke with a start. It was the third time this had happened in a month. The police seemed useless in stopping it. She flinched as the doorbell rang persistently, abrupt and rude in the silence of the night.

'Come out here and talk to me, you bitch!' a man shouted, followed by a violent thumping at the door.

Katy remained still in bed. It was as if he could see her through the walls. She'd changed the locks, and the windows were double-glazed and secure. There was no way he could get in, but fear gripped her entire body.

Louis was a prick, a Class 1 prick. She'd left it far too long before she confronted the issue, probably because she knew that this is how it would end. Badly. There was no telling the man it was over. He was an arsehole. There was no way she was spending her life with him. She'd wasted enough of it with him already.

At first he'd seemed charming, handsome and sexy. Louis was hot, there was no other way to say it. Yet again, she'd allowed her worst judgment to get the better of her. He was educated, a lawyer in the City, well-groomed and sharply dressed, and a man over whom other women drooled, but that didn't stop him being a violent, jealous idiot.

It took some time to be revealed, as it usually does. They'd met in a bar, and Katy had been a little worse for wear. She and Emma had been out on the razz – short skirts, tits out, the lot. She knew it wasn't clever, and that she was doing womankind a disservice, but sometimes a girl needs to get laid, and that's how she'd felt that night.

Louis showed more interest in Emma at first. His hand had been glued to her waist after he'd placed it there casually while they were all chatting and she hadn't thought fit to remove it. But as they spoke, it became clear to everybody in the group that it was Louis and Katy who were sleeping together that night. Emma was out of the picture, she'd have to settle for his greasy mate or go home alone.

Even as Louis was going down on her, Katy despised herself. How had it come to this? She was in her mid-thirties and still jumping into bed with idiots. She thought back to a conversation with her dad earlier that week.

'When will I be seeing a grandchild?' he had asked. 'I won't be around forever ... especially now.'

Probably never, she thought, as Louis worked his way back up to her lips. She could tell even then that he was a vain, superficial tosser, but he had all the right parts. She'd thought that well-toned stomachs like that were only photoshopped onto models – she didn't realise they could be for real.

Screw it! she thought as his hand moved over to his wallet to pull out a condom. I'll stop this soon. Soon I'll find somebody like Elijah ...

She banished the thought to the back of her mind. It had been nineteen years ago and they were kids back then, but she'd never met somebody she'd loved as much as Elijah. Would they have made it? Perhaps they'd have got married and had a family. By now she could have been a frumpy old woman ravaged by the demands of motherhood. Who knew? They never got the chance to find out. And if her experiences of men since had been anything to go by, Elijah had been the only decent bloke in the entire world. All the others were wankers. At least the ones that she'd met.

She knew that she had to change this pattern of behaviour: unsuitable men, never relationship material, and always ending in tears. Was it her fault? Did she attract them? No, it was never her fault. No woman turns a guy into an aggressive idiot. That's his choice. But she had to admit that she might be attracting them. Perhaps it was a signal she was giving out – guilt, perhaps, culpability even.

Katy acquiesced as Louis began to deliver some accomplished moves below the sheets, her thoughts dispersing, encouraged by the bliss of a man who knew exactly what he was doing in bed. She shut that mental door and left her convictions safely on the other side.

That had been three years ago. And now here he was hammering on the windows and leaving her a petrified wreck once again. She hated herself for it. She despised herself for sleeping with him in the first place. She'd known it was wrong and that it wouldn't lead anywhere, but she'd done it anyway.

The wonderful, regular sex and the initial over-attentiveness of Louis soon resulted in him moving in. That was when the bad behaviour started: the questions about who she'd been drinking with after work; the Spanish Inquisition whenever she stayed on in the office; the smell of perfume on his jacket when he arrived home late at night after an evening working on a case. Or so he claimed.

She knew that he was sleeping around. She saw that his behaviour was threatening towards her. He was controlling and spiteful. He hadn't hit her – yet – so she convinced herself that it didn't matter. It was psychological, not as bad as physical violence. That's what she told herself. But she knew the drill. It started with mind games and it would end with violence. But when you're caught up in it, it doesn't happen all at once. It creeps up on you and you don't see it coming. Then when you realise what's happened, it's too late. You're stuck in there. It takes a monumental effort to begin the change. And Katy simply didn't have the energy for the inevitable confrontation.

Then he hit her. Sure as houses, it came. There was no bruise, not one that anybody would see beneath her clothes. She'd challenged him one night when they were all out together, accusing him of fancying Emma. After all, it had been Emma he'd been chatting up right at the beginning.

Of course, he denied it. Katy was pretty sure that her best friend wouldn't do something shitty like that, but she wasn't imagining it, Louis was flirting with her. Emma wasn't reciprocating, but Louis was provoking her, trying to get a rise. Well, he got it alright. Katy threw her drink over him in full view of their friends and stormed out. As she exited the bar, she heard him laughing it off. Some joke about it being her time of the month. Wanker.

He followed her out, all smiles, the epitome of a concerned boyfriend. Then, when he'd caught up with her, he pulled her into a side alley.

'You ever embarrass me like that again, you bitch, and I'll break your fucking neck. Understand?'

He had his hand around her throat, his face was right up to hers. He was furious, out of control.

'Understand?' he shouted again.

Katy nodded, tears in her eyes. She was trying to be strong, but it was terrifying. What could she do?

His other hand slammed hard into her stomach, not in a fist, but with so much force that she doubled up and couldn't stand straight for quite some time.

'Now, let's go home,' Louis said, once she'd steadied herself. 'Your tits look great in that dress. Let's not put them to waste, eh?'

At that moment she knew that it had to end. She couldn't put it off any longer. There was no more kidding herself, no more explaining it away. She'd sensed this was coming and she should have ended it before it happened. She felt ashamed. She was an educated woman, for Christ's sake. Someone like her shouldn't end up being the victim of domestic violence.

In her youth she'd scolded women on the TV countless times, shouting things like 'Why don't you just bloody leave him?' and 'I'd have been out of there ages ago!'

Well, as she'd discovered, it wasn't as simple as that. Louis was like a tick. He'd burrowed into her life and he wasn't getting kicked out without a fight. Katy didn't get it. If he hated her that much, and he really seemed to, why didn't he go away and find some other woman to terrorise?

This was the middle-class face of domestic violence, a sharply dressed lawyer and an accountant. They were affluent, outwardly successful, and to everybody looking in at the relationship, a modern couple who had everything going for them. But he was a shit and Katy had to get him out of her life. She was ashamed and humiliated by how far she'd let things run, but she'd sort it out first thing on Monday morning. She'd get the locks changed and she'd throw him out. It was her house – he was renting out his place still. It wasn't as if they were engaged or married or anything like that. And thank God they hadn't got kids.

A shower of pebbles hit her bedroom window and jolted her out of her thoughts. Picking up her mobile phone, she pulled the quilt off the bed and made her way to the cupboard on the landing. Taking the key from the lock, she activated the torch on her phone and ducked into the small space. She closed the door behind her and locked herself in from the inside. The torch turned off, she drew the quilt over her head, then stuck her fingers in her ears to drown out the sound of hammering at the door. Either the neighbours would call the police, or he'd give up, eventually. Either way, she'd had enough. This had to end.

'How are you feeling? You look much better.'

She was lying. He looked terrible. Worse than last time.

'I'm alright, darling. Just having trouble with my memory. I can't seem to sort my thoughts out. It's like someone gave my head a good shake and jumbled everything up.'

Katy squeezed his hand. She loved her dad. She couldn't understand why she chose such unsuitable men when she'd had him as a role model all of her life.

'What are the doctors saying now?'

'The usual,' he replied. 'It was another stroke. A nasty one. It's knocked me for six, I can tell you.'

She thought back to the earlier TIAs. Like Louis's inevitable punch, this had been coming for a long time, but what could they do? Terry had had to sit it out and wait:

monitor his blood pressure, take the blood pressure pills, have another aspirin. Katy felt helpless. She couldn't even wire a plug with any degree of confidence, let alone make any recommendations about how to deal with her dad's medical problems. They were in the hands of the doctors. They had to follow their advice.

'How's it going with that young idiot? Has he backed off yet?'

Katy didn't want to trouble her father with it. She'd let it slip shortly before he was rushed to hospital. For all she knew, hearing what had happened with Louis is what had pushed him over the edge.

'It's fine, Dad. I think he's got the message.'

He hadn't, of course. But Katy couldn't possibly tell her father that. She'd been huddled in the upstairs cupboard, terrified for her life. Louis had been pounding at the door, thumping the windows and shouting horrendous threats through the letterbox for at least an hour before one of the neighbours chased him off.

The police came soon afterwards. With her fingers still in her ears, Katy had been too exhausted to move. It didn't help that they thumped so hard at the door she thought it was Louis back again. A policeman's knock they call it. Well, in the middle of the night it's downright frightening.

She didn't move for half an hour. She was too scared. They pounded down the door in the end. It made a complete mess of the frame, but they thought she might have harmed herself, apparently.

'Do you want to make an official complaint?' they'd asked.

'Will it make any difference?' she replied. 'It hasn't done so far.'

The problem was, he hadn't hit her again and he

hadn't threatened her directly in public. There was nothing for the police to get their teeth into. Not yet. It was more mind games. He knew he could paralyse her with fear – he didn't need to hit her. How long would it go on? Surely the bully would move on and find another target soon? Katy was passing him on for some other poor woman to deal with. She was too spineless to sort him out herself, so she would hide from him until he got fed up, and then some other female would go through exactly what she had done. She simply didn't have the energy for the fight.

'I know you're lying,' came the reply. 'I can see it in your face. You never were a good liar. I could always tell.'

'Look, Dad, I know you're worried, but I'm okay, honestly. It's being handled. You need to get better, don't worry about me. Just get well again, okay?'

'You know we always loved Elijah. The minute you brought him home at Easter I said to Sue, those two are made for each other. If they don't marry, I don't know anything about relationships. And as we got to almost forty years together, I'm at least partly qualified to say something like that.'

'I know, Dad. Talk about coming on heavy with him. I think he was scared that you wouldn't let him leave the house until he'd proposed. We'd only known each other a term – I was eighteen or nineteen. I can't even remember properly. Eighteen, I was still only eighteen then. What do you know about relationships at eighteen?'

'I met your mum when I seventeen, and we were married by twenty. That's how you and Elijah would have been. If he hadn't ...'

'I know, Dad. We were young, who knows what might have happened? But it's over, it's a long time ago now. I thought I was in love with Elijah back then, but I can hardly remember it now.'

Katy watched as her dad's eyes began to tear up.

'What, Dad? What is it?'

'I'm sorry, darling. I'm so sorry, but they don't come to ask me often enough. They leave me here and my legs are still too shaky to get out on my own.'

'Oh Dad,' she said, moving over to put her arms around him. 'It doesn't matter. You can't help it. Please don't let it upset you.'

She held him tight. She could smell the urine through the sheets. This man who'd once been so big and strong to her, it was humiliating for him to be like this. Weak. Defenceless. At the mercy of nurses who were too busy to give him the care that he needed.

'I love you, Katy. You know that, don't you? I'm so proud of you. I know things haven't always gone right for you in your life, but I never doubted you. You were always my little girl. You'll find someone who deserves you one day. You'll get your happiness, don't you worry.'

A nurse walked up to the bed, sensing that something was going on. Katy didn't want to stress her dad, but she unleashed her anger anyway.

'Can you please take care of your patients properly? He's been here on his own for hours and nobody thought to bring him a bedpan. What do you think he's going to do, for Christ's sake. He's had a stroke.'

'Okay, Ms Wild, calm down please, we'll take care of this. I'm sorry, Terry. You should have pressed the buzzer, you know what it's like in here.'

She beckoned to another nurse who pulled the curtains round the bed to give him some privacy from the other patients.

'I'll be outside, Dad,' Katy said, wanting to spare her father what little dignity he had left. There was a flurry of activity behind the curtain, and all Katy could hear was the constant apologies of her father to the nursing staff. Sorry for the trouble. Sorry for making a mess. Sorry they were having to clean up after him.

Katy sat on one of the plastic chairs outside the cubicle and waited for them to finish. It was time to make changes in her life. She couldn't bear another night like that. She had to move, maybe even away from London, certainly to a place where Louis wouldn't be able to do what he'd been doing. She couldn't let him carry on like that. Enough was enough, she was shaking things up. She would change her job, move away and start again.

Then, to her side, panic and activity.

'Page Doctor Flynn!'

'Dad? Is he alright?'

She could tell from the nurse's face that he was not.

'You're going to need to stay here, please,' she replied. 'He's having another stroke.'

'Oh no ... Dad!' Katy pleaded, but stepped to the side, letting the professionals get on with their job.

It was only ten minutes. That's all it took to lose her father. Technically he was still alive for those minutes, but once the stroke had occurred it was only a matter of time. As far as Terry Wild was concerned, life ended in that hospital bed. There were scans and discussions about the possibilities of surgery, but he didn't make it. The bleeding was too great.

'It was a haemorrhagic stroke,' the doctor had explained. Katy didn't care, it was all superfluous now. She'd lost her mum to cancer three years previously, and now she'd lost her dad to a stroke at only sixty-two years of age.

The nurses let her sit with Terry for a while, but it soon became clear that they needed to get on with whatever happens when someone dies in hospital. Katy held his hand, it wasn't even cold yet.

'We need to get your dad moved, darling. I'm sorry. You'll be able to see him later. They'll make him look nice for you.'

Katy didn't need him to look nice, he was her dad. He looked peaceful. She hoped it had been quick.

'Would he have been in pain?' she asked. 'Is it a peaceful death when you have a stroke?'

'It was quick. It happens very fast and I don't think he would have known what was going on.'

'Did he say anything?' Katy asked. 'Did he speak to you when it happened?'

'No darling, he was just muddled – he kept saying the same thing over and over again. Something about how he did ring the buzzer.'

Katy moved the wine glass round and round in her hand as Emma scolded her.

'You'll knock that over if you're not careful,' she said, touching Katy's hand to discourage her.

'Now you're about to put it all behind you, how do you feel?'

'Drained. And tired.'

'It'll soon get better. You've had a lot of horrible things happen recently. You're doing the right thing, you know, but I'm going to miss you.'

'Well, it's not over yet, by a long stretch. You're still

meeting me in Inverness on the Sunday. That's your half-term then, isn't it?'

'Yes, yes, it's fine. I'll see you there. Mind you, it's such a long way to travel by train. It takes over nine hours. Nine hours! I could fly halfway around the world in that time.'

'You of all people know why it has to be in Inverness. I have to go back there before I move on to Europe. It feels like something I have to do.'

'I know, I know. You are going to be safe on your own, aren't you? You are taking care?'

'It's rural Scotland, Emma. What do you think it'll be like? Rapists behind every tree? I'll be safe. I'll let you know on Facebook. It's fine.'

'How are you feeling about your dad?' Emma asked, squeezing Katy's hand again.

'I'm okay,' she replied. 'We gave him a good send-off. He's back with mum, and they'll be having a good old laugh again wherever they are now. I miss him though. I miss him so much. It feels like there's nobody left.'

Katy fought back the tears. She didn't want to cry. She was sick of talking about strokes, funerals and death.

The only consolation about losing her father was that Louis had cooled off. He'd left her alone. Perhaps it was Terry's final gift to her. He'd managed to see off the idiot who was ruining her life.

'I'm sorry, I didn't mean to bring it all up again, but it doesn't go away either. I don't want you to feel that you can't say anything now the funeral is over. If you want to talk about him, you can bang on as much as you want. I knew them both for a long time too. I've been seeing your dad on and off since ... well, since we were at university, almost twenty years.'

'Bloody hell, we're old buggers,' Katy laughed, shaking

aside her thoughts. 'How did we end up like this?'

'We're no different from anyone else. Everybody has terrible relationships these days. Your dad and Sue, they were lucky, like my mum and dad. I don't know what they fed that generation, but they make marriage look so easy. I guess they didn't have Tinder to distract them back then.'

'Nor did we when we were young. Mobile phones were just coming in when we were at uni. I couldn't even afford one until after I'd started work – they were dead expensive then. Besides, you could only make a phone call on those old Nokias. You certainly couldn't swipe right for a shag!'

They laughed. It helped Katy to forget everything when they did that.

'I wish I was as brave as you,' Emma said, serious all of a sudden. 'I hate my job. Teaching, for fuck's sake! How did I end up teaching? I despise those spotty teenagers. If they had as much brain power as they do acne, our nation could be great again. They have no interest in learning. I don't know how the hell they're going to pay for their mobile phones and laptops when they're adults if they can't even be bothered to get out of bed and come to school in the morning.'

'Dad left me a bit of money, and with the sale of the house – it won't be much, but it'll be another ten thousand in the bank – I reckon I can last two years on my own with zero income. I'm not an accountant for nothing, you know. I've done the spreadsheets. But I hope it won't come to that. I'm sure I can pick up accounting work on the way. If not, I'll only be thirty-nine, I'll be able to find another job by the time I'm forty. Besides, I'll be married to some nomadic digital tech entrepreneur by then.'

More laughter, more swigs of wine.

Two well-groomed men walked up to their table, full of

themselves. Katy clocked them and quickly assessed that the dark-haired one was wearing more hair product than she and Emma combined.

'Hello girls, how are ya doing?' asked Mr Cocksure.

'Sorry boys, married!' Katy said, waving her hand at their suitors.

She watched as the guy's face dropped.

'I'm still game if you are?' he chanced.

'Much as we're tempted, we've got to go home for our cocoa,' Emma chipped in.

They took the hint and pushed off.

'Where did you get that?' she burst out, the minute the men were out of earshot.

'It's my mum's,' Katy smiled. 'I found it in some of the stuff that Dad left me. I'm putting it all into storage. I reckon I'm going to get a lot of that when I'm hiking on my own. See, it works. Scares 'em off every time.'

'You're good!' Emma laughed. 'I wouldn't have thought of that. What a shame it won't keep that jerk Louis away too. I can't believe I was jealous of you that night you copped off with him. I dodged a bullet there. Though his mate was terrible too. He was wearing Fred Flintstone boxers. I chucked him out when I saw those. I refuse to have sex with a grown man in Fred Flintstone boxers!'

Shit, we're shallow. Maybe that's why things are so bad.'

'Well, it all stops now,' Katy replied.

'Yeah, right!'

'I'm serious. When I spoke to that counsellor guy, he reckoned it all goes back to what happened in Scotland. Unresolved issues, he said. I agree with him. I've hidden from what happened for too long. It's not right for a woman of my age to still be getting it so wrong with men. I'm changing. I'm sorting out my life.'

'I'll bet you five quid you can't keep off sex for two years,' Emma said.

'It's not the sex, it's the relationships. I'm not getting into any more relationships like that, not until I'm sure. Louis is my last dickhead. I've learned my lesson. I'm telling you, no more idiots.'

'Good luck with that,' said Emma, finishing off her wine. 'What time are you leaving tomorrow? Can I see you off?'

'Of course you can,' said Katy, consulting the emails on her phone to pull up the times.

'I leave Euston at a quarter past nine. I've got to go over to the storage unit with the removal guys first and get my stuff locked up and hidden away. Will you drop the key into the estate agent's for me? I'm not going back into the house. The council will take my dad's place back as soon as I'm out of it. The bastards wanted it last month, but I managed to play the bereavement card. The post is all sorted too. You sure you're okay to forward it on to me? It'll be a pain in the arse, but I'll owe you one.'

'Of course I'm happy to take your mail. And you've been a pain in the arse for almost two decades, there's no reason to stop now.'

So there it was. Their last drink before Katy headed off on her backpacking adventures. Her job was gone, the house on the market and what was left of her and her father's possessions all neatly stored in boxes. It felt as if her past was all bundled up and ready to pack away. But it wasn't. There was still something left. After all those years the one thing that she would have liked to have locked up and packed into storage was still out there. And it would soon be coming back to haunt her.

CHAPTER TWO

May 1999 'Bollocks to the Student Loans Company. The next thing you know, they'll be making us pay all of our fees.'

Sarah was ever the conspiracy theorist, convinced that the government was out to sabotage everything. Nathan had not yet had the youthful idealism kicked out of him. His parents topped up his student income, and he even had a car, so the new loans system was only a curiosity for him.

'No way!' he replied, stirring the large pan of beans that the friends were about to share.

'How's that toast coming on?' he asked, managing to mix his politics with culinary duties. 'Besides, nobody would ever accept paying over five thousand quid for fees.'

It was a heady cocktail of cheap food, naive politics and sexual manoeuvring in the student kitchen. They'd been in the halls of residence for over two terms and the Easter break was just behind them. They weren't yet living in close enough proximity to begin to loathe the sight of each other. There would be plenty of time for that when they moved out into shared houses, and the fighting over fridge space, lack of toilet paper, and bathroom hogging began for real. For now, it was all friendly. They could still retreat to their separate rooms if things got a bit tense, and in any case they were spread over several halls. Of course, that meant a feast such as the one they were about to enjoy took some coordination.

Isobel walked into the communal kitchen accompanied by Emma. Their faces were red. They'd only had to climb two flights of stairs to get there, but they looked as if they'd been halfway across the city rather than along to the local corner shop.

'Booze!' they shouted together, as if they'd rehearsed it beforehand. Livin' la Vida Loca came on the radio, which had been playing quietly in the background. Katy leant over to turn it up and the room burst into a spontaneous show as the six teenagers performed their best dance moves while the beans began to stick to the bottom of the saucepan.

Another student called Neil popped his head around the kitchen door, saw what was going on and thought better of it. He'd be eating late that night, or resort to the chippy. There was no way he was cooking in there with that bunch of wankers messing about. Besides, he'd tried his luck with Katy at a recent Student Union disco and she'd rejected him. Nicely, she wasn't a bitch or anything like that. But he was still reeling from having plucked up the courage and been given a knockback. It would take him some time before he recovered his dignity and tried again with another woman. Not all students tumble into bed with each other. For people like Neil, it was something they were obliged to watch from the sidelines.

'These beans are disgusting, Nathan,' said Emma, swigging a plastic cup filled to the brim with cheap white wine.

'It's because this wine doesn't complement my fine

menu. Everybody knows you drink red wine with baked beans.'

Emma flicked a bean off the side of her plate towards him, and it hit him directly on the forehead.

'You cow!' He lined up three of the crispy beans which had been scraped off the bottom of the saucepan and flicked them: one, two, three – a barrage of military aggression, embroiling a neighbouring country by the name of Elijah. Grinning at Katy, he joined in the food fight, which swiftly escalated into a full-blown global conflict. Within five minutes the kitchen table was splattered with food debris.

'Shit, we'll lose our deposits if we don't clear up.'

'It's alright for you, rich boy. Mummy and Daddy will pay,' said Sarah, never one to miss a pot-shot. 'Some of us will have to sign a Faustian pact with the Student Loans Company just to be able to keep eating shit like this.'

'Either way, we'll need to clean up,' replied Elijah, ever the peacemaker. He knew that Sarah was only trying to get a rise, and if nobody took the bait she'd be laughing and joking with the rest of them in no time at all.

'It's not my hall of residence, so no skin off my nose,' Nathan chipped in.

Isobel moved to the kitchen door, blocking it.

'Nobody leaves here until my deposit money is safe,' she said, concerned that they were about to evacuate the area and leave it in a state. She could be really fussy about the cleaning.

Elijah crouched down, reached into the cupboard and brought out some rather sparse cleaning supplies.

'Right. Emma and Izzy, you clear the table. Sarah and Nathan take the floor, and Katy and I will wipe the walls. And when we're done, Mummy and Daddy will treat you all to fish and chips. You deserve it, some of you have never cleaned a kitchen before.'

In that single exchange, Elijah demonstrated why he was such a popular member of the group. Not only had he placed Sarah with Nathan – he knew that she fancied him, she was almost eating him alive – but he'd also put Emma and Izzy together, and so managed to win a coup for himself and Katy.

They weren't sleeping together yet, and there was much conjecture among the group about whether they were an official item or not. They'd done the sensible thing. Katy was now on the pill and they'd got pretty close to full-on sex. He'd even met her parents over Easter. But he really liked her, he was her first, he wasn't going to rush her. Being a gentleman was all well and good, but his balls felt like they were about to explode. He hoped it wouldn't be much longer.

Elijah was generous with his money too. He knew that people like Sarah and Katy had bugger-all. They didn't get financial top-ups, their parents couldn't afford to make up their money, so it would be inevitable that they'd take out student loans. A treat like fish and chips made all the difference when you were broke. In spite of his privileged background, he understood that, and he helped whenever he could. He didn't want to provoke Sarah's more militant tendencies, but she'd accepted his offer without protest. Even political idealists have to eat.

Half an hour later, the room was filled with the aroma of fish. The wine was flowing, the kitchen clean – or passably enough not to get a warning from the warden – and the food was good.

'You know, we should go away together in the summer

holidays. We could get a holiday cottage or a lodge. It wouldn't have to cost a fortune.'

Nathan looked at the faces around the table, waiting to see what reaction he'd get. He'd been thinking about it for some time. He'd got his eye on someone, and it would be an opportunity to get a bit closer, although he wasn't certain that his interest was being reciprocated.

'That's a brilliant idea,' Katy chimed in first. 'We're not going to see each other for weeks over the summer. It's going to drive me mad having to spend it all at home. Let's do it!'

She leant in towards Elijah as she spoke. He was taking a puff of his asthma inhaler – the combination of booze and cleaning products had made him wheezy. There were still several weeks to go before they all went their separate ways, but already she couldn't face the idea of having to be apart from him. They lived at different ends of the planet, or so it had seemed at the time.

Izzy chimed in.

'I can't do it. I'm working at my mum's shop over the summer. She thinks she might have to close if we don't have a busier season this year. I can't let her down.'

'Why don't we stay up near you?' Emma suggested. 'You can come and visit. Scotland is the perfect place to go on holiday. We could even camp up there if it's too expensive to get a house. What do you think, Izzy?'

She nodded in assent. It would work like that – in fact it would liven up her summer. Since her dad had left, she knew how precarious the village shop had become. He was generous enough with her, but a right bastard to her mum, and now she was at uni there was no obligation for him to support her anymore. Izzy feared it was already too late for the Bonnie Prince Charlie Highland Store.

It wasn't long before the fish and chips had been demolished and a rough plan drawn up for the long summer vacation. Elijah knew the area well, as did Isobel. They were going to look at a place near Spean Bridge, which was close enough to Fort William but still out in the wilds. There was a cinema at Inverness where they could get their fix of city life, rural Scotland style, if they were going stir crazy out in the wilds.

Elijah and Katy were in charge of booking and decided to pick up brochures from the travel agent's the next day. Elijah had resolved to subsidise the rental for everybody – he'd make sure that nobody was financially embarrassed. They'd never know. He'd divide up the costs and present them with a bill which was at least seventy-five pounds light. He wanted this to happen, his parents were loaded – embarrassingly so, as it had turned out when he began to mix with a greater variety of people at uni. He would do his bit to spread the wealth about.

Katy was delighted that they were going into town together the next day. She'd taken the prerequisite number of contraceptive pills to make sure that pregnancy was no longer a risk. She was feeling tiddly from the wine and hot for Elijah. It was happening that night. She'd decided it was high time she and Elijah did the deed.

Katy's armpits were clammy and she was tired now. Who could have known that her dad had kept so much junk? She'd cried a lot that morning. She'd thought that she was getting there – yesterday she'd almost managed her first full day without getting choked up at the thought of his death. She'd already airbrushed into oblivion the bit about him lying in a pool of piss when he died. She couldn't quite cope with that, it made her indignant and she didn't want to feel angry when she thought about her dad.

He'd told her how proud he was of her. She could see that as she sorted through the pile of rubbish that he and her mum had saved from her childhood. There was the Christmas angel she'd made at primary school when she was five. It was her first Christmas at school and she'd been so pleased with herself. It was a toilet roll tube covered in now-browning tissue paper, with a face drawn on in crayon and a hairpiece made of cotton wool. It looked to Katy more like the Elephant Man than the Angel Gabriel, but her five-year-old self must have been delighted with it.

Why had her mum and dad kept all that old stuff? She was surprised that her dad hadn't thrown it out when her mum died. He'd got rid of a lot of bits and pieces then. He was angry about her cancer. Her dad had never been a man to get cross, but she'd seen real fear and fury in him when the cancer began to get aggressive. Maybe he'd needed to hang on to the memories – perhaps too much of their lives was rooted in those boxes of primary school artwork to be able to throw them away.

Katy had hired a skip and it was now almost full, positioned on the roadside in front of Terry's house. She'd booked a small van to take the important stuff to the storage unit. The removals men were coming over to her dad's after clearing out her own house. She was never going back there again.

She'd had a tip-off from work that Louis had been asking for her at reception. They'd done the data protection thing and informed him that they couldn't pass on personal information about employees. He'd begun to kick off, of course, but they had CCTV in the reception area, and Gloria was great. She'd seen off her share of pricks in her time greeting the public and answering the phones. That and the fact that Katy had told her what was going on, so whatever yarn Louis tried to spin, they were not going to give him any clues about where she was living. This was her chance. If she could only get away on the train to Scotland, and then to Europe after that, she'd be able to start again and reinvent her life.

Had her mum and dad been proud of her? She was not proud of herself. Sure, she'd got her degree, moved into accountancy, progressed steadily through the endless exams and qualifications. She'd earned decent money – it never seemed to go far enough, but she was doing alright. In any case, lots of women were single at her age, that's how it was, but she still felt she'd let them down.

She'd never quite managed to recapture what she'd had with Elijah. They were kids, and it probably would have come to nothing anyway. After they'd starting sleeping together, they couldn't bear the idea of being parted over the long summer break so they'd split the holiday, flitting between his house and her house, with two weeks spent with their friends at the holiday lodge.

They'd started the holidays at her home, in her mum and dad's council house. It was a lovely estate. Terry kept the garden looking beautiful, and they hoped they'd be able to buy the place soon.

Katy had never been embarrassed about her life until she went to Elijah's house. It was huge. His dad was an entrepreneur and had started investing in mobile phones – for all the good that would do him, or so Katy had thought in 1999. He'd made money on property in the past, flipping wrecks that he'd renovated: buying homes from distressed owners and then selling them on at a profit. It had got tense over dinner one evening when the penny dropped and Katy realised that Elijah's dad was buying up homes from people like her parents, people who had bought their council homes, discovered the realities of home ownership – fluctuating mortgage rates, broken boilers and blocked pipes – and had to relinquish the houses that they'd dreamed of owning for so long when the financial realities set in.

She and Elijah had been together for barely seven months. It had been smouldering for ages, but her thirty-seven-year-old self wondered if you could even call it a relationship at that age. Her parents loved Elijah immediately and completely. He was not snobby or judgmental in any way, and he got on well with Sue and Terry. She often wondered if Elijah was uncomfortable about his dad's money. The irony of his girlfriend living in a council house can't have been lost on him.

Her dad and mum, with the confidence of a couple who'd racked up thousands of air miles in their own relationship, told Katy that he was 'the one' within twenty-four hours of meeting him. Katy thought she loved him too, but he was the first boy she'd slept with, and for all she knew it might only be infatuation. She had no experience to base it on, but it had felt like love at the time, and she'd never felt anything like it since.

Katy came across a shoebox packed with photographs and began to sift through them. They were blurred and generally of a poor quality – cameras had been so bad when she was younger. They were almost embarrassing to look at these days when cameras on phones allowed even people like Katy, with no artistic skills whatsoever, to take a decent picture.

She worked her way through the collection. Most of them you'd delete on your computer, but occasionally she'd stop at one and a wonderful memory would come back to her. Some of these photos were hers. She'd forgotten about many of them. They were taken around the time she was at uni. She'd got to a stage in her life, after graduation, when she'd asked Terry and Sue to look after the pictures for her. They were too painful for her. She'd decided to make a fresh start. That was the first of her fresh starts and she was still making them sixteen years later. The truth was, she could never move past that summer. She wasn't sure if any of them had.

It had seemed such a great idea at the time. That damn holiday, it ruined everything. If only she'd taken up Elijah's dad's offer to shack up in one of his rental houses for the summer, everything would have worked out fine. But she couldn't do it. Sarah's voice kept ringing in her ears, banging on about how the previous tenants had been evicted and that she and Elijah would be benefiting from somebody else's misfortune. Even Elijah wasn't comfortable with it, in spite of the wonderful prospect of being able to shack up together for an entire summer rent-free.

'Some tax dodge my dad has dreamed up,' he'd said. 'Don't worry, he'll be making money from it somehow.'

Well, screw student ideals. Elijah's dad was still alive and had made a fortune from his small chain of mobile phone stores. They'd been bought out by some massive company and he'd retired at fifty-two years of age, lucky bugger. But his son was dead, and all because they couldn't swallow their pride and live in that bloody house for the summer.

Katy came to the university photos. She hadn't seen them for years. It was like a chronology of a disaster that was yet to take place. She wondered what they'd been thinking when the pictures were taken. They'd had no idea what was coming. Then, there he was – Elijah. What would he look like now? He'd no longer have those boyish looks. Katy had already noticed that gravity was fast becoming her number one enemy. But Elijah was a good looker. She'd seen pictures of his dad. He still had a full head of hair, and he looked good for a guy of sixty or thereabouts. It was probably all that cash.

And then she came to the photos of the holiday. Most of them were Polaroids. The colour was dodgy, the pictures faded. Elijah had bought her the camera for her nineteenth birthday earlier in the summer. It must have cost him a fortune. The entire saga, right up to Elijah's death, was captured in that pile of images.

There was the sound of a horn outside. The removal guys had arrived. Katy hesitated over the Polaroids for a moment, then slipped them into her bag. She'd examine them later. This was no time for avoidance – she had to confront the past. There was a knock at the door and she got up to let the men in. This was the last time she'd ever be in her father's house. She was closing doors, and this time they had to stay shut.

***

'Izzy's got back to me. I thought she'd gone into hiding.'

'Good. Is she up for it?' asked Katy, checking her own phone for messages. Nothing there. It was the small things like that which kept reminding her that her dad was gone. He used to text her all the time.

'Yes, she's fine, says she can't wait.'

'Tell her I'll be sending her a friend request now she's on Facebook – if I can remember how to do it. I can't believe it took her so long.'

'While you mention it, I want to take a look at your

settings. You're bloody useless at social media. You still haven't sorted out your privacy settings, have you?'

'Well, we – you – blocked Louis. He can't see what I'm up to now, so I didn't think much of it.'

'What's to stop him signing up under some other name and stalking you that way? Your profile is still open. Any old nutter can perve over you. Look, give me your laptop and I'll do it before you go. How long have we got?'

'The train boards in twenty minutes,' said Katy, looking at the departures board. She reached into her rucksack and pulled out her laptop. She'd splashed out on a new Mac, only because it was so light and thin. She'd had a dry-run with her bag the week before and failed dismally. She'd found a great YouTube video showing how to travel light. She was now Katy Wild, owner of five pairs of undies, two bras, six pairs of socks, two T-shirts, two pairs of jeans, a light dress and a shirt. She was wearing a lightweight fleece, which had cost her way too much but was made of some super fabric which prevented sweating and could also protect her from a second Ice Age, or something like that.

She'd bought the Mac, kept her old phone and tooled up with a couple of currency cards to make sure she could always get hold of some cash. She'd thrown in some sanitary products for good measure, congratulating herself on her Girl Guide preparedness, squeezed in a packet of plasters in case of blisters and loaded up with travel-size packs of toiletries. That was her life, jam-packed into a bag which could be carried on her back. Everything else was either in storage, in a skip, or on sale in a charity shop. Katy was amazed at how little she really needed.

Emma took the laptop, fired it up and locked onto the free wireless from the bar opposite.

'You sure you don't want a drink?' she asked. 'For old

time's sake? It seems rude to steal their broadband without buying anything.'

'No, I'm good,' Katy replied. 'They have some sort of lounge on the train. I'll have a drink there while we're travelling. I haven't a clue how much sleep I'll get on that thing.'

'You are a dope,' Emma cursed as her fingers ran across the keyboard. 'You've got this lovely bit of tech and you haven't got a fucking clue how to manage your privacy settings. Everything you do is public. I told you about this. How are you going to keep Louis out of your hair if you can't get this stuff right?'

For a moment Katy was pissed off with Emma for having a go at her, but reluctantly realised that she was right.

'Look, I'm changing your settings to *friends of friends* and your posts to *friends only*. That way only people you want to be in contact with you can get in touch. Fuck! Your profile is on public too. Right, that's getting changed. I'll change your old posts, make sure weirdos can't contact you from your phone and email and you're good to go.'

'I haven't got a clue what any of that means, but thank you. I will still have some friends, won't I?'

'Yes, but only the ones you want, none of the creeps. Present company excepted, of course.'

Katy was going to miss Emma. They'd been friends for years, even more so since Emma had got a teaching job in London and they'd managed to meet up regularly. It was a familiar friendship, a shared past. Relationships like that mature on the vine, they don't appear overnight. Strangely, they'd got to know each other better in the years after university.

What was she thinking of? She'd never been backpacking before. In her student days you went Inter-Railing, if you did anything at all. She'd never been alone in the wilderness and she hated being on her own, but in her more soulful times, she'd realised that it was the time alone that she needed. She'd used life's distractions to hide from her problems. So it was scary as anything, but something she had to do. And it had to begin with going back to where it started, the place where everything had gone wrong: Scotland, Spean Bridge, the one destination she'd avoided since Elijah died.

Katy figured that if she could put those ghosts to bed at the start of her journey, it would be the ideal kick-start to changing her life. If things went well, she might never have to come back home.

'I'll have to be going soon,' she said, looking at the departures board. 'These sleeper trains board early, I think.'

'Never done one,' Emma replied. 'Not until I join you next week, unless I chicken out and fly up to Inverness. Oh, Nathan and Sarah contacted me. They can meet us for lunch on the Monday. They're catching the train from Aberdeen. Nathan wanted to avoid Sunday because the trains are always crap. He's travelling away for work this week. He's a handy guy to be back in touch with. He fixed my tech really well, spent a few minutes messing around via some app and it was all good as new. You should let him take a look at yours. Anyway, I said yes to meeting on Monday. Is that okay?'

'Yes, of course. It'll be good to see them. I haven't had any meaningful exchange with them for ... well, for ages.'

'Cool. No mentioning kids, by the way. It's a touchy subject. Sarah didn't sound very happy when I spoke to her. I think things are a bit tense.'

'I always thought it was weird how those two got together so quickly after Eli— You know, after that summer.

I know Sarah always fancied Nathan, but his mind was elsewhere. There's something odd about them, about Nathan in particular.'

'That sounds like one of Sarah's old conspiracy theories. It's hilarious how much of a Tory she became after her radical student years. Still, I suppose we've all changed. My tits are definitely beginning to droop. I'm thinking of marking it on my stomach like you measure kids' heights against door frames. I'm sure I'm not imagining it.'

'We can have a race to see whose tits hit their waistline first. A fiver says it's me by the time I'm fifty.'

'Hey, I know what I meant to tell you. I found some photos of Scotland when I was sorting through Dad's stuff. I brought them with me to see if they'll help us work out where we stayed. It's funny to think that we didn't have internet back then.'

'Ooh great, let's have a quick look at the pics. I haven't a clue where it was. I looked on Google Maps, but that Little Chef has gone since we were there. I remember it was nearby, and we were up some farm track – there's no way that'll be on Google. You'd need a bloody satellite to find that place.'

'Izzy should know. I'll ask her when I get connected with her on Facebook.' Katy handed over the photos. She hadn't had time to rifle through them herself, they were tucked into a compartment in her bag.

'Wow, these take me back. Look at your hair ... look at my hair! Look at everybody's hair! How did we ever think that was a good look ...'

Emma was choked up suddenly, her eyes reddening.

'God, it still gets me. I'm sorry. Look, take these. I don't want to spoil your send-off by getting more tearful than I feel already. Show them to me next week. I'll be prepared by then – I hadn't expected that to be so emotional. You'd better make a move.'

Emma nodded towards the departures board. The train was boarding. At that time of the evening Euston was as quiet as it ever gets. It felt strange to be at a station so late. Katy replaced the Mac in her bag, fastened it and slung it over her shoulder. It was light enough. She'd done well, she could manage to carry that weight all day.

'I'm going to miss you, Katy.'

'You'll see me next week, you silly old moo.'

'No, not that. I'm going to miss you being here in London – after next week. I love you, you know.'

'I know, I love you too. I'll be back, and you can come and join me anytime. Just hop on a plane. We'll meet up at half-terms and holidays, you'll barely know I'm gone.'

'Fuck!'

Emma stopped dead. The train was ahead of them, people were boarding and it didn't look too busy.

'What? What is it?' Katy surveyed the area.

'Duck into the side a moment and I'll tell you.'

Emma moved Katy in front of the train where they could no longer be seen along the platform.

'I told you to sort out your bloody Facebook settings, and now look what's happened.'

'What?'

Katy was oblivious to the source of this sudden tension.

'It's Louis, for Christ's sake. He's waiting halfway along the platform. He's looking for you.'

CHAPTER THREE

July 1999 They probably should have called it quits when they realised how remote the lodge was, but youthful enthusiasm and a simmering cauldron of teenage emotions made them press on. By the time they arrived, they were tired, hot, hungry and stiff. Five hours cramped in a small car weaving left and right, up and down, on the roads along Glencoe had been like the world's worst big dipper and both Sarah and Emma had had to step outside to throw up. It had sounded like fun when they were planning it back at uni.

If only they could have fast-forwarded a decade or so to the invention of sat nav. Elijah's out-of-date AA road map had got them to the rough vicinity of the holiday lodge, but even the locals didn't know where it was. They'd stopped off at the Little Chef in Spean Bridge for food and a toilet break, but they were a good hour driving along farm tracks looking for the lodge.

'Thank God for that. We're here!' Katy exclaimed.

As Elijah's girlfriend, she'd got the passenger seat, while Nathan, Sarah and Emma were crammed in the back. Izzy was joining them on her moped the next day. Katy could feel the festering resentment and thought her comment might convey a bit of empathy, but it wasn't she who'd had to throw up because it was so damn uncomfortable in the back. Sarah had got stuck with the lingering smell of vomit for the past couple of hours, and Katy had lost her goodwill when she put the air blowers on full at the front of the car.

It was a good job that the lodge looked like it did in the brochure. It was built entirely of wood. There was so much wood, it was more wooden than a tree, which at least has a few leaves thrown in for good measure. Wood walls, wood floors, wooden furniture – even a wooden roof. Still, it was surrounded by forest, so it made sense in a roundabout way.

As the friends stepped out of the car and stretched their legs, the mood began to lighten.

'The key is where they said it would be,' Sarah announced, lifting the round stone to the side of the front door. She opened up the lodge, walking straight into the kitchen–living area. There was a box on the kitchen worktop packed with provisions from the local shop: cereal, teabags, bread, beans. There was milk, margarine, wine and beer in the fridge.

'I know the journey was shit, but you can't complain about the service. They said they'd arrange a delivery from the nearest shop and they have. Everything is in here, so at least we don't need to go out again tonight,' said Elijah.

He was always the glue in that group. He had the ability to bring them all back together. Nobody had thought to thank him for doing all the driving, they'd been too busy bitching about their own discomfort. But Elijah just got on with it.

He was looking forward to this break. He and Katy had had to endure a week at his parents' house, after moving on from Terry and Sue's place to pick up one of his dad's cars for the road trip. They'd been in separate bedrooms out of concern for his younger sister's moral wellbeing. He'd only just entered the paradise of a stable and exciting sex life with his first proper girlfriend when the tap was suddenly turned off. And his parents wondered why he had a face like a wet blanket all week.

He was dying to grab a room, make his excuses about being tired and get Katy into that double bed. They had a week's worth of sex to make up for, and he had no intention of being seen before midday the next day.

In a sneak preview of what was to come when they moved out of university accommodation into their student digs, the disputes over bedrooms began straightaway. It had always been accepted, by Elijah and Katy at least, that they would get the double bed. After all, they were the official couple and Elijah had subsidised the trip, even though the others weren't aware of it. Worse still, they were a bedroom short. What had been classed in the brochure as a bedroom, was really a small office space with a Z-bed folded up in the corner.

Nathan cracked open the beers and a passive-aggressive version of the Lord of the Flies began, with each of the friends willing to eat the others to get a decent place to sleep. It was a bloody negotiation and became more so as the booze began to flow. It metamorphosed suddenly when Nathan proposed a game of strip poker to determine a victor. They were tiring of the row by that stage and the suggestion of a boozy game of poker came at exactly the right time.

By midnight, Elijah and Katy were fast asleep in one of the single rooms, with not an aching ball in sight. Emma was tucked up in the double bed, wearing only her knickers.

That was the sign of her victory over Nathan who'd left the room naked. Sarah had hung around, her modesty carelessly covered by a large cushion from the settee. The way she saw it, Nathan had lost because she kept dropping the cushion to reveal a glimpse of nipple. She'd get him into the sack if it was the last thing she did. As for Katy and Elijah, they'd been first out of the game. That was by mutual agreement. Katy wanted to get into Elijah's pants as soon as humanly possible, and the poker game obliged by meaning they both had their kit off already by the time they headed for bed.

Tempers were much sweeter in the morning when Izzy arrived. Used to negotiating Scotland's rural charms, she'd experienced none of the difficulties of the previous day in locating the lodge. She seemed relieved to be among her friends again, away from the oppressive austerity of home, and that meant she was happy to share the double bed with Emma, given that they seemed to be a room down.

Isobel's arrival was what they all they needed to move on from the squabbles and bitching about the room alloca-tion. Before long, Elijah had been out to the local shop, returning with frozen pizzas, beer and wine. They were all sitting in the living area as if they were back at university. It was like old times before the end of year exams when they hadn't a care in the world. Life was good. They had their digs sorted out for the next academic year and were busy planning the holiday, talking about what they'd do when they were up in Scotland.

Sarah was resolved to finally bed Nathan, who seemed to have some prudish resistance to her. Well, she'd soon fix that. The poker game had been only the beginning, and if he'd been excited by a flash of nipple, wait until she got him behind closed doors. She might seem obsessed with politics, but she had physical needs like everybody else and Nathan seemed the guy to oblige. She couldn't wait. With any luck the smile on her face would soon be as broad as Katy's. As for Emma and Izzy, they seemed happy to be there among good friends and away from their parents.

In the unlikely event that anybody passed by the lodge, they would have heard laughter, joking and tomfoolery. They might have smiled to themselves, chuckling at the sound of friends having a great time and putting their money into the local economy.

But if that's what they thought, they'd have been deceived by those sounds, because inside that lodge a toxic cocktail of frustration and jealously was beginning to build up. When it finally exploded, a young life would be lost.

'How did he know I would be here?'

'I told you, it's your Facebook settings.'

'But I unfriended him, like you said.'

'Did you block him? And it doesn't matter anyway, your settings were all on public so he could see what you were up to without friending you. The entire world could see. I'm surprised there aren't more people here to wave you off.'

Katy felt stupid. Emma had been ranting at her for ages to sort this stuff out. When she was telling her how to do it in the pub it had all made perfect sense, but the next day, when she sat at her computer with a hangover, she could never remember the details. And now here was Louis, arse-hole of the year.

'What should we do? If he sees me, he'll kick off.'

'What did you post on Facebook?' Emma asked, her face barely concealing the anxiety she was feeling. She'd thought she was seeing off a friend. With Louis on the platform, things were going to get difficult.

'Look, Katy. I need to give you these,' Emma said, reaching into her bag. 'They arrived this morning – the postal redirection is obviously working.'

'That was quick,' Katy replied, scanning the envelopes and looking ahead to check on Louis's whereabouts. She stuffed them into her pocket. There were more pressing matters to deal with.

'Go into the first carriage and sit in the first seat that you find, on the opposite side of the platform. He won't see you until the train starts to move and, with the reflections in the windows, he probably won't spot you even then. I'll stay out of the way, and if he looks like he's getting too inquisitive I'll distract him. He hasn't seen us yet, so if we keep out of sight he'll assume you've changed your plans.'

'Love you, Ems,' Katy said, moving forward and embracing her friend. 'See you next week in Inverness. Don't mess it up, make sure you're there.'

Emma held Katy tight. She admired her friend for what she was doing. She'd considered throwing in the towel with her own job and joining her on the trek, but she had to give a term's notice as a teacher. It was like a prison sentence, aimed at trapping them in the career forever. She was too spineless to call their bluff and walk away from the job she hated, so she settled for the half-term visit to Inverness.

'Go,' she said. 'I'll keep an eye on tosspot over there. British Transport Police should be around somewhere. I'll give them a shout if it all kicks off.'

Katy picked up her rucksack and took a final look along the platform for Louis.

'Shit, he's gone.'

'Get on the train. I'll look for him. Check your phone – I'll text you.'

Katy stepped on the train and followed her friend's advice, taking the first seat that was free on the opposite side of the platform. She moved over to sit by the window, placing her bag on the seat beside her. There was activity outside. It looked as if they were getting ready to leave.

A young guy with a huge rucksack walked up the carriage from the farthest entrance, scanning the area for his seat. He seemed to be accustomed to the business of heavy duty walking. For a moment Katy wondered if she'd bitten off more than she could chew.

There were a couple of businessmen in the carriage, with a smattering of sharp-dressed women. Long days for all of them, no doubt, and now an even longer journey on the Caledonian sleeper. A retired couple were both reading novels. He had a Tom Clancy, hers was a Mills and Boon.

Suddenly, she saw Emma's face at the window. She'd been working along the carriage from the outside looking for Katy. She was gesticulating down the train. Katy didn't need to interpret the hand signals, she could already hear the commotion in the next carriage. Louis had come on board and was checking the seats. The train staff had asked him if he was travelling and he was now holding up the departure of the train. As with most things related to Louis, it had suddenly got tense.

'Keep your bloody hands off me. You touch me again and I'll sue you for assault.'

'Please calm down, sir. We need you to step off the train please. We have to depart on time.'

'I need a few minutes to find my ... wife ... I have an important message for her that can't wait.'

He burst into Katy's carriage. The tension was immediate as the occupants braced themselves for conflict. Would they have to intervene or not? Could they keep their heads down and let it all work itself out?

Katy tried to blend into the background, but she could see Louis checking the seats methodically, pursued by two smart and well-groomed staff. It was bizarre how she clocked their Highland-style uniforms in spite of the impending confrontation.

'Where are you, you silly bitch. I know you're here somewhere.'

Katy's stomach knotted. She'd thought that she was free of the idiot, and now he was here to spoil her last moments before making her escape. She shuffled in her seat, turning towards the window. As she did so, the two envelopes that Emma had given her slid out of her pocket. One was from the Inland Revenue. What a send-off! Louis and the tax man there to wave her goodbye. The other had a computer-printed label on it. It wasn't corporate, it looked like it had been sent from a home address. She wanted to open it there and then, but sensing Louis at the seat behind her, she stuffed the mail deep in her pocket and pulled up the hood on her jacket.

'Found you, you bitch!'

Katy held steady, facing the window.

'Sir, that's enough. If you don't leave this minute, we will have to ask the police to escort you from the train.'

It was the female assistant who spoke. Instinctively and with well-practised contempt, Louis thrust out his hand and pushed her away. She stumbled and fell into the aisle, bumping the young trekker in his seat as she did so. The colleague who was with her stepped back, shocked by what he'd seen, and not at all certain that he dared to tackle this idiot.

Katy turned so that Louis could see her face. She didn't want the staff to take any more of his nonsense. She'd need to confront him.

'Piss off, Louis. I've told you it's over.'

'It's not over until I say it is. What do you think you're doing? Do you really think you can run away from me?'

'You drove me to this, Louis. I don't want to see you again. Accept that it's over. It ended the moment that you hit me in that alley.'

Katy was half-aware of something going on behind her, but she was watching Louis's clenched fists. It was like looking at a bomb which was about to explode.

'I'm taking you off this train and we're talking. You know I didn't mean to hurt you. I told you I'd had too much to drink. I love you, Katy ... we're meant to be together.'

'For Christ's sake, Louis. Do you really think I'm coming back to you? I stayed far too long. It's over. Leave me alone. I don't want to see you again.'

'Well, you don't get a choice in that—'

'Excuse me, mate.'

Louis was caught off-guard. He wasn't used to being interrupted. He expected to be listened to. He turned around, his face bright red.

'Fuck off!' he screamed at the young guy who'd stepped on board with the rucksack.

The young guy smiled at Louis and turned to the other passengers, addressing them as if they were his audience.

'You heard that, right? You saw what he did to this young lady?'

The man nodded towards the train assistant who was now sitting down being comforted by the Mills and Boon lady. There was a murmur of agreement.

The young guy's fist came out, hard, fast and sure. Louis dropped to the ground like a brick.

'My nose!' he squealed. 'You broke my nose!'

'Apologise to these two ladies,' the young guy said, calm and cool.

'Fuck you!'

The young guy stepped up to him as he lay on the floor and struck him a second time.

'Apologise to these ladies,' he said once more, completely relaxed, as if he did this every day.

'Soddy,' came the nasally reply. Louis's nose was streaming blood.

'Now fuck off!' the man said.

Louis took one look at him, as if he was considering a final challenge, but thought better of it. He began to crawl along the aisle, then stood up and placed his hand on the carriage door.

'I dow where you're goin,' he muttered through his bloodied nose. 'Don think thid is ober, you bitch!'

The cavalry arrived in the form of a British Transport police officer who looked like he'd stepped out of an episode of Heartbeat. It was a good job that a hot pursuit hadn't been required, he might not have been up for it. Louis was escorted from the train. The tension eased immediately and there was a round of applause for the young man who'd had the courage to see off the idiot.

He smiled, made a little bow and then turned to Katy.

'Oliver Harris,' he said, holding out his hand.

'Pleased to meet you.'

'Thank you so much for doing that,' Katy said, feeling

immense relief that Louis had been taken off the train. If she could have inflicted such heavy damage on him herself, she would have done so a long time ago. At last, a bit of justice in the world.

Of course, Louis had been ranting and raving about legal action, assault and ruining careers as he was removed from the carriage. The usual nonsense from a powerless bully. It didn't seem to perturb Oliver at all.

'Your knuckles are bleeding,' Katy observed. 'Here, I've got a tissue somewhere.'

'I've never done anything like that before,' Oliver replied. 'That guy sparked something in me. What is he, your husband or something? Okay if I move your bag?'

Katy nodded and Oliver stowed her rucksack between the backs of the seats. She caught sight of Emma waving at her from the platform as the train began to move. She'd completely forgotten about her in all the commotion. She waved back, hoping that she would be able to see from that distance. She could see that Louis was shouting something at her. It didn't take much imagination to figure out what it would be. The word bitch would be in there somewhere – and some bollocks about getting his revenge. Poor Emma, she might get some hassle herself now that Louis knew she'd been on the platform. She fumbled for her phone to send a text, but Oliver had moved her bag and was asking if it was okay to sit in the opposite seat.

The male train assistant, who looked incredibly grateful for Oliver's intervention, returned from the bar area with some ice for his knuckles.

'Can I get you anything from the bar?' he asked, 'as a thank you for doing that. I thought things were going to turn nasty there.'

Oliver looked towards Katy, prompting her to order first.

'I'll have a glass of red wine, if that's okay. Thank you.'

'A lager for me,' Oliver replied, taking his seat.

The female assistant was still shaken, but had been taken away by a more senior member of staff. There was an air of gratitude in the carriage – it had been some start to a long journey.

'He's my boyfriend, by the way,' Katy said as he settled in the seat and ran an ice cube over his knuckles. 'Ex-boyfriend. He's a bloody liability. You might not have done anything like it before, but you certainly sorted him out. Thank you.'

'I'm still shaking, to be honest with you,' Oliver smiled. He was handsome, with a bright, friendly face. He had a confidence about him, but it wasn't arrogance. He was comfortable talking to women, and there was no hesitation as he struck up a conversation with Katy.

The drinks arrived. Katy took a larger sip of wine than she should have. She needed it.

'Steady,' Oliver said. 'We're not even out of London yet!'

The alcohol immediately put Katy at her ease. She'd already forgotten to send that text to Emma.

'You stood up to him really well. Somebody should have done that a long time ago.'

'Where are you headed? Call me Olly, by the way, not Oliver. I don't use Oliver, it sounds so bloody posh.'

'Fort William,' Katy replied. 'I'm walking the Great Glen Way.'

'To get away from that arsehole?'

'Pretty well. And everything else in my shitty life. I'm

going to travel the world. I'm selling up and seeing what happens.'

'Wow, good for you!' Olly replied. 'Put it all behind you, ditch the ex and make a fresh start. Did you leave a job?'

'Prepare to be underwhelmed,' Katy replied after taking a second large sip of wine. 'I was an accountant – well, I still am. I'm going to work on the road now. Wherever I lay my hat, that's my home.'

'An accountant? That's boring! I thought you were going to say you did something exciting, like being a librarian or an archivist. You really know how to do adrenalin, don't you?'

He smiled. He was charming, naturally so.

'Piss off!' Katy laughed. 'So what is it that you do that's so interesting?'

'I don't have a job as such. I do internet stuff – selling T-shirts online. With funny slogans. Hilarious things like *No Wi-Fi? It's time to move out!* and *Old People's Tinder. Matches Required!* You get the gist: ironic slogans for millennials. I can't believe they sell either, but they do.'

'Brilliant!' said Katy, impressed. She slipped the wedding ring off her finger and into her bag. Maybe she wouldn't be needing it that night.

Tom Clancy man came up to them and leaned over the table to talk conspiratorially.

'Jolly good job there, son. Thank you for sorting out that idiot. I'd have done the same myself had it been twenty years earlier. The world needs more people like you.'

'No problem,' Olly smiled, holding up his hand. 'You don't know how to sort these out, do you?' His knuckles were no longer bleeding, but they looked sore and red.

'They'll feel stiff in the morning, but they'll ease up soon. You only hit him twice. Keep using the ice.'

'Great,' Olly replied. 'Thank you.'

Tom Clancy man went back to his seat. His wife had resumed reading her Mills and Boon. The business passengers were at ease, happily continuing their discussions about the problems with the boss, the inefficiencies in the office, and how they'd get it all sorted out if they were in charge.

'How does that work then?' Katy picked up. 'Do you keep the T-shirts in your backpack?'

Olly laughed again. He was nice. He wasn't sneering at her, it was rather that he'd found her question endearing. She wished Louis had been capable of that.

'I take it you and the internet don't get along too well. I do it all from my laptop. I get them drop-shipped and the money goes into my Paypal account. I travel all over the world, like you're about to do.'

'I'm not that bad with web stuff,' Katy replied, 'but I wouldn't call myself an expert. I'm going to have to get better at it because my entire business will be run through my Mac from now on. How cool am I?'

'Can I check your tickets please?'

The conductor had reached them.

'Are you both okay?' he asked. 'Thank you for doing what you did. Fiona is a bit shaken, but she's very grateful to you for helping out.'

Katy located her ticket and handed it to the conductor.

'I hope she's alright. I guess you don't get a lot of trouble on these sleepers. Hang on, I'll get my ticket,' Olly replied.

'You're in berth 11L,' the conductor told Katy. 'You can access your room now if you want to. You're lucky, you've got it to yourself, it's a quiet night.'

Olly handed over his ticket.

'You're in the seats, but if you want a table in the lounge this evening, that's fine. I'll let the steward know there's no problem. And don't worry about that idiot. If he tries to take any legal action, we'll say it was self-defence. We have a zero tolerance of violence on board. We'll back you up, don't worry.'

He moved back along the carriage.

'So, you're in the posh seats,' said Olly. 'You won't keep that up for long, not once you've been at this for a while. Cheap seats make the money go further.'

'I still have money left from working, so I'm safe for quite a while. I thought I'd treat myself. At least I didn't go First Class, that might have been too indulgent.'

'Well, enjoy!' Olly smiled. 'It's a great experience, these sleepers are amazing.'

'I'd better find my berth and sort myself out,' Katy said. 'Want to join me in the lounge later on and I'll buy you a drink?'

'Yeah, why not. Is ten too late? That gives you twenty minutes. Is that okay?'

Katy nodded and stood up. She picked up her backpack from the space between the seats and started to make her way towards the door.

'See you later!' she waved, smiling at the other passengers as she walked along the carriage. They had a connection now, since they'd all been involved in the earlier altercation.

Katy hadn't had time to take in the environment on the sleeper train. It was similar to a regular train, but with elements that you'd also find on a ferry. There were more places to sit, and the cheap seats, as Olly had called them, were wider with more room to stretch than usual. The lounge looked amazing, it was very inviting. It had the feel of Air Force One, or at least the portrayal of it on TV. It was a regular bar–restaurant fitted into a narrow space. Katy loved it.

She found her berth. It was a tight fit in there, and she was pleased she wouldn't have to share the room. It gave a better feeling of space without the upper bunk lowered. After a few minutes she'd got herself organised. She perched on the narrow bunk and checked her phone. Emma had sent her a text.

Lucky escape! L was really kicking off after they took him off the train. Wanker. You're well rid of him. Sorry he messed up your departure. Be good, Em x

Katy sent a reply. It was good to hear from Emma though she hadn't even been gone an hour.

Dead right he's a wanker. It's over now, I'm free of him. Thx for helping, sorry it turned to shit. Missing you already :-) K xxx

As Katy went to return the phone to her pocket she felt the crumpled envelopes that she'd rammed in there earlier. She took them out and studied each one in turn. The HMRC one was a notification about her final tax from work, nothing to worry about. She hadn't thought out what she was going to do about any letters she received on her travels. Normally they would have been tucked into a filing cabinet at home. She took a photo of it with her phone, and then tore it up into tiny pieces and dropped them into the small bin that was tucked under the sink. She wouldn't be able to gather clutter on the road. She'd need to use paperless options for storing notifications like that.

It was the other envelope that was intriguing her. As an accountant she was primed to open the HMRC brown envelope first, and with that out of the way she studied the more interesting letter. It was definitely printed at home. She was no expert but it looked like the smudged print of an inkjet printer rather than the sharp professionalism of a corporate laser model.

It was a London postcode: E11, Leytonstone. She didn't know anybody who lived there. Katy tore it open. Inside was a single piece of white printer paper folded neatly into quarters. The paper and envelope were mismatched in size – this was definitely a personal note. Nobody ever wrote her letters anymore. Who could it be from? She unfolded the paper and scanned the note. There was no address and no date. Just a short, printed note, short and sharp.

You're to blame.

CHAPTER FOUR

July 1999 Things settled down after that first night. Nathan did the best thing possible by suggesting a game of strip poker. It diffused the tension straightaway. It's hard to be angry when your pals are chanting at you to rip your pants off.

What followed was a reasonable holiday, punctuated by the odd bit of tension or manoeuvring. At least that's how it appeared on the surface.

The transport arrangements weren't perfect, and on more than one occasion Emma hopped onto the back of Isobel's moped to free up some space on the back seat of the car. It seemed clear to everybody but Nathan what Sarah's intentions were and they wanted to give their friend a bit of space to see if she could close the deal.

Emma didn't have a helmet, so she'd arrive at their chosen tourist location for the day with her hair all over the place and having swallowed at least two flies along the way. It was a constant source of amusement to the others and she took it in good spirit.

That part of Scotland was fabulous and they enjoyed

working through the brochures and leaflets in the lodge, deciding on where they would visit one day at a time. The sights of the Glenfinnan Monument, Inverary Jail, Oban and Mallaig kept them suitably entertained, and by the time they got back home in the evenings they were ready for a night of beer, crisps and laughter.

But on the day that Elijah died, none of them had been laughing.

It had begun that morning. In a replay of what they jokingly referred to as the Student Kitchen Massacre of 1999, Isobel had got intense about the state of the kitchen once again. This had made the atmosphere prickly as they all set off on that day's trip, a long ride out to Eilean Donan castle. Elijah was a big fan of the movie Highlander and of the rock group Queen, so for him it was a must-see attraction.

Things began to go awry from the outset. Sarah was sick again – all over Nathan's lap. The constant weaving in and out of the passing places on the narrow road they'd taken following Elijah's so-called shortcut had proved too much for her stomach. She was furious, more so at throwing up over the object of her desires than at being travel-sick.

Isobel was annoyed with everybody again, because she'd managed to race ahead on her moped and she and Emma had been left at the entrance to the castle wondering what was keeping their pals. The two girls had argued while they were waiting and things were definitely frosty by the time they'd all regrouped.

Even Elijah was out of sorts. That was unusual. He was the most even-tempered of all of them, but he'd finally snapped. This was the only trip that he'd insisted on making throughout the holiday, and Katy had been taking the mickey, doing impressions of Freddie Mercury singing

Bohemian Rhapsody. Nathan and Sarah joined in, and before he knew it he was in the middle of a Wayne's World reprise. Well, it pissed him off. So what if he liked Queen and was annoyed whenever anybody parodied them? All he wanted to do was enjoy a day out, see where they'd shot the opening scenes of the film and admire the castle.

He reached into Katy's bag, which was resting at her feet. He grabbed his asthma inhaler, taking two puffs. He'd worked himself up. He'd felt his chest tightening as he got angrier, but this was his favourite group that he was defending. They were worth it.

All in all, by the time they got back to the house that evening it didn't feel like they had a lot in common. Elijah and Nathan had gone off together leaving the girls to do their own thing. Izzy didn't want to be with anybody, so avoided the castle and went exploring on her moped. Without putting it into words, that was a 'Get stuffed' to Emma, who would now be consigned to the back seat of Elijah's car if she was going to get home. She'd be sandwiched between Nathan and Sarah, some seriously frustrated sexual tension, and the smell of old vomit.

Sarah, Emma and Katy explored the castle. They each had someone to bitch about.

'He takes that bloody pop group so seriously. It was hilarious when you and Nathan came in with the Galileo bit, I nearly wet myself laughing.'

'I can't believe Isobel. I know she's fed up with her fascist mum, but there's no need to bring that Brethren bullshit on holiday with her. First it's the state of the kitchen, then it's ... well, she's in a foul mood today, we're best steering clear of her.'

'What's wrong with him? I've all but hopped on and helped myself, he just doesn't seem interested? Do you think he's too much of a gentleman? I'm getting desperate here. I never expected to have to finger myself all holiday.'

And so it went on. Three angry friends, nobody listening to each other, all impatient to be heard.

On her own, three miles away at a scenic picnic ground, Isobel was thinking darker thoughts, but with nobody to temper her anger.

In spite of being deeply in love with Katy, Elijah couldn't move past his anger at her. He felt she'd betrayed him. She knew how much he loved Highlander and she of all people knew how he treasured his collection of Queen CDs. By ridiculing him in front of his friends, she'd attacked the very essence of him. She wouldn't do that if she really loved him, would she?

Nathan had other things on his mind, and had done for a long time. He was relieved to be spending some time alone with his friend. He got what Elijah was saying about the music. Katy had been a bitch and he regretted joining in with the singing. He'd make it up to Elijah. He started by apologising. He was pleased to get a break from Sarah. He knew what she was after, but he needed to check something out beforehand. He wasn't certain yet, but if he was reading the signals right, he'd soon put her out of her misery.

Nobody could have known it then, but the touchpaper was set. It only needed to be lit. When all the elements came in place, it would play out like a well-rehearsed dance.

When they arrived back at the lodge, the friends split off and ate separately. Izzy had been home first, way ahead of the others. They knew she'd got there first because there was a newly filled bin bag in the dustbin. She was tense when they came into the house, greeting them only to let them know that she was there. She picked up her book and retired to the bedroom which she and Emma were sharing. It was clear she was in no mood to talk.

Elijah had infuriated Katy by allowing Nathan to ride in the front of the car on the way home. It was a public snub and Katy hated him for it. There would be no cuddles that night. Time to teach Elijah a lesson. The bubble had burst. It had been some time coming, but this was their first relationship crisis and both of them recognised it as such.

Katy and Emma stayed in the lounge while Elijah and Nathan grabbed a couple of beers and sat on the Z-bed chatting. Out of her mind with frustration at Nathan's behaviour, Sarah went off to sit out at the back of the lodge, taking a pile of old magazines to read.

And so it was for over an hour after they returned from that fateful visit to the Scottish castle. And if anybody was observing from afar, they would have seen the precise moment when choices were made and events turned on their head.

The house was quiet. Sarah had moved back inside and was reading at the dining room table. There were murmurs from the bedroom as Nathan and Elijah chatted, and Emma was dozing on the settee. Katy was looking out of the window watching the light begin to fade and feeling angry about how Elijah had humiliated her. The more she thought about it, the angrier she got. He would have to apologise. She wasn't going to let it drop.

Izzy was still on her own. She'd come out to the kitchen to make a cup of tea, but remained tight-lipped. She stepped outside onto the patio to enjoy a cigarette.

Then, out of nowhere, Nathan could be heard shouting. Elijah's voice was also raised. There were more angry words. Nathan stormed out of the room, slamming the door. He muttered something to Katy who snapped back at him.

Emma was jolted out of her doze and Sarah looked up from her magazines, wondering what the commotion was all about.

Within half an hour, Elijah would be dead and Katy would be sorrier than she'd ever been in her life. Three people would have played their part in the tragic death of a young student who'd been looking forward to enjoying some time over summer with his friends.

Katy had known she was going to sleep with Olly as soon as they started chatting in the lounge bar. The letter had shaken her, and she needed the company. Besides, he was hot and much younger than her. They'd never see each other again after the train journey, so what did it matter?

Only, it did matter. This was the reason she'd packed in her job and decided to travel the world. It was time to leave the bad choices behind and make a fresh start, but it seemed the past still wasn't done with her.

She hadn't got much sleep on the train. She and Olly had met up in the bar as planned, and she'd set about the red wine straightaway. Already a little light-headed from their earlier drink in the carriage, it wasn't long before they were laughing away at Olly's adventures backpacking. It was an entirely new world to her, but for Olly it was his life. He related stories of terrible toilets in Thai hostels, deadly insects in sleeping bags and a list of stomach complaints that made her resolve only ever to drink bottled water when out of Europe. But the way Olly told it, it made her laugh. He wasn't that much younger – thirty-one – so it didn't feel too weird hooking up with him. He probably had a girl in every port, and she'd be another tick in a box, alongside a night in Bangkok or Seoul.

He stirred next to her. It had reminded her of Elijah in those bloody university dorm-room beds. They were three feet wide and a devil to share with a boyfriend. The beds in the sleeper train were even narrower. Sex had been more like working through a set of IKEA instructions than the passionate and reckless affair that she'd have preferred it to have been.

Still, it made her forget the letter for a while. When she'd read it, she'd wanted to tear it up and throw it in the bin alongside the debris from the HMRC notification, but instead she'd stared at it for ten minutes, wondering who might have sent it, and why now? Perhaps Louis really had been following her Facebook posts.

Katy surveyed the debris on the floor. Her knickers had got caught on the door lock when she'd thrown them to the side. She couldn't have managed that on purpose if she'd tried. The condom was stuck on the sink cover where she'd pulled it out and thrown it aside. At least Olly had come prepared. She hadn't packed condoms. She'd get some in Fort William. She hated the bloody things but at least they'd help her stay healthy.

She considered moving. Her back was stiff. She was closest to the edge of the bed, and she couldn't believe that she hadn't tumbled out onto the floor. At least there was a pile of clothes there that would've broken her fall. She was naked and a bit chilly. She could feel Olly's breath on her neck. One thing about younger men, they didn't snore. Louis had made a racket at night.

Katy stretched her arm out to pick up her phone, which was dangerously close to the condom. She reached out gently, trying not to wake Olly. She wasn't ready for the morning-after conversation yet – she hadn't decided what she thought about it. Was she a cradle-snatching slut who'd jumped into bed with the first young guy who'd made her laugh until her knickers dropped to her ankles, or was she an empowered modern woman who was entitled to make the choices that made her happy?

Olly shifted in the bed, but didn't wake up. She'd breakfast with him if he wanted it, and then make her excuses when the train drew into Fort William. If he seemed clingy, she'd pretend she needed to take a taxi to her next destination, and that would create some quick separation. With any luck he'd be polite and friendly, and then get lost as soon as they arrived.

She touched the screen on her phone and it kicked into life. There were several updates including a picture of somebody's dog wearing a bobble hat and scarf. What the fuck? People bang on about animal rights, but don't animals have the right not to look like bloody idiots on social media too? Katy clicked through the drivel, and then read Emma's reply to her text.

Somebody filmed Louis on Twitter. Check your feed. Bloody hilarious, the wanker. Can't really see your face, the joke is on him. Good journey? Em x

Katy had given up posting on Twitter some time ago, and had actually managed to make her account private with Emma's guidance, but she could still check out what other people were doing. Emma was right. The video was there for all to see. Their public episode of domestic violence had already garnered 6012 likes, 3489 retweets and a clutch of not very cerebral comments from casual observers who were happy to make sweeping statements based upon a short extract of their altercation.

There were the usual thoughtful comments such as

Wanker lol, #Twat and *Mike Tyson? Sorry, just some other a-hole!* Then there were the obligatory woman-haters who were always looking for an opportunity to come out and play: *Looks like she deserves a good thump!* and *Shut up and get the dinner on luv #slut.*

Katy had read enough. She watched the video again. You couldn't see her face – thank goodness she'd pulled up her hood when she'd heard Louis. Nobody would recognise her unless they knew it was her. One of the business-people must have filmed it. That must have been why they were all too busy to step in and help her out.

Olly opened his eyes. Katy cursed to herself. It was time to talk.

'Morning sexy!' He ran his hand along the back of her leg. It felt good and for a moment she considered going another round with him in case a sexual desert lay ahead, but she thought better of it. He was hot, but she didn't want to invite any more hassle into her life. One shag means nothing, coming back for seconds the next morning – well, that's almost going steady.

She made her excuses and rolled off the bed, placing her feet on the floor.

'It's a really snug fit in there,' she said, evading Olly's quite obvious intentions. She could see the outline of his erection through the sheets.

'Oh, you mean the bed?' he smiled, offering her an opening line to talk back sexy.

No, she wasn't going to sleep with him again. She caught a glimpse of her neatly trimmed bush in the full-length mirror on the door. That wasn't going to last long on the road. It would be down to her knees in no time. Shaving one's intimate areas was one of the first luxuries to go, according to the travel blogs.

Olly had one more try.

'You were dynamite last night. I didn't know that position was even possible. It's amazing how inventive you can get in a small space.'

Katy batted it straight back.

'I'm really hungry. Any idea how breakfast works?'

'Okay, fair enough!' Olly replied, finally getting the message. Katy hooked her knickers off the door lock and pulled them up her legs.

'We've got an entire week together, there's no rush.'

Picking up her bra, Katy did a double-take at Olly's last words.

'I beg your pardon?'

'I just said, let's take it easy. I get it. It's a long walk, we have all week.'

'You didn't think you were coming with me, did you? I want to do this walk on my own.'

The mood had changed. Olly's erection was long gone.

'Oh ... I thought as we slept together last night ... we've been getting on so well. I thought we could walk the Great Glen Way together.'

Katy berated herself. Were all men pricks? What was it that made them think that sex gave them automatic proprietorial rights? She needed to sort this out, and quickly – assertively – so she didn't end up with another Louis on her hands. She fastened her bra and pulled it down over her breasts. She needed to be covered up to say what she needed to say.

'I'm going to be very clear about this, Olly. I'm grateful for what you did to Louis last night, I really am. And I know we spent the night together and it was fun, but I am not walking the Great Glen Way with you and this is nothing more than a casual encounter. You're a nice guy. Really. But this is it – it's a one-time thing. Okay?'

Olly nodded. At least he wasn't the type to kick off like Louis. He looked at her, and then sat up on the bed.

'Fair enough!' he replied. 'Sorry if I got the wrong end of the stick. But you know we'll see each other again, don't you? There aren't that many places to hide on a walk like that. We'll run into each other sooner or later.'

Katy had never used Airbnb before, but how hard could it be? She figured it was just Tinder for rooms and guests. She was bound to find a match. She left Olly in bed and sneaked off along the corridor to the toilets to cancel her hotel booking. The male and female facilities on the train were placed next to each other and some guy was grunting in the cubicle next to the one she was about to enter. She hadn't a clue what he was doing and didn't particularly want to know. She'd spotted a more spacious unisex cubicle further along the narrow corridor, so opted for that instead.

The sleeper had been okay, she suspected, because she'd been out cold after a satisfying sexual encounter with Olly. As one-night stands go, it wasn't bad. He was confident and funny, he knew what he was doing and he understood how to use the rhythmic undulations of the train to both of their advantage.

But that line about seeing her on the Great Glen Way? That was right out of the stalker's handbook and she was shutting it down straightaway. She cancelled the town centre reservation, registered on Airbnb, and found a nice looking place outside Fort William. She had a feeling that

Airbnb was going to become a close buddy on her travels around the world.

Emma had made her promise that she'd let her know where she was staying and when she arrived. A simple safety precaution for a lone female traveller, she had said. Katy forwarded her the confirmation email.

Olly was too cool to eat breakfast, so Katy ate alone. She gazed at the magnificent scenery as she ate her bacon roll and nursed her cup of tea in the lounge bar. She saw Spean Bridge flash by. It wasn't long before they would arrive at their destination.

Spean Bridge, the place where it all turned to shit. They had been so young. There was no way any of them were equipped to deal with what happened. She hadn't even experienced the death of a relative at that age – it was her first death and her first funeral. None of them knew what to do. She did a lot of growing up in the weeks following the loss of Elijah.

Katy fumbled for her phone, thinking that she should send Emma a photo to let her know that she'd arrived. She couldn't find it. Cursing, she took the last sip of her tea, and then made her way back to the toilet she'd been in earlier. It was engaged. She didn't have to wait long for the flush, followed by the sound of the hand drier.

'This yours?'

Olly stepped out of the cubicle with two phones in his hand.

'I recognised the bling.'

He handed Katy her phone.

'Thanks,' she said, cursing what a clumsy cow she'd been to leave her phone in the loo like that. It wasn't the first time she'd done it either.

'Looks like we're here now,' Olly smiled. 'Thanks for last night, it was good. I had fun.'

He stretched out his hand. He seemed fine. This was it, they were shaking hands as mates. Acquaintances. And she would always be grateful to him for what he'd done to help her in the carriage.

'Look, thanks for chasing Louis away yesterday. I really appreciate it. And I enjoyed last night too – it was fun – but you do understand it was a casual thing? Nothing serious.'

'Yes, yes, of course,' Olly nodded. 'Nothing serious, no worries. It was great meeting you. I hope you have an amazing adventure out there.'

The train pulled into the station. Olly had his bag with him already and he was off like a whippet from a trap. Katy went back to the room to gather her belongings. She thanked her lucky stars that he hadn't been difficult about going their separate ways. For a moment she'd begun to question her ability to spot a decent man.

Paige Hudson was a bit scatty and had a house full of cats. Katy hadn't read that bit in the Airbnb description, she'd only done a superficial check of the blurb. In fact Paige was the archetypal cat lady. Divorced, no children, living on her own. She was desperate to care for somebody – anybody – but with nowhere to direct it. Her cats got the benefit of her personal frustrations in life and she talked to them as if they were human beings. Katy liked Paige from the moment she answered the door.

'Welcome to Solus Na Madainn!' she smiled, holding a cat which Katy later learned was called Mr Depp. After Johnny Depp. Paige named her male cats after her favourite

TV and movie stars. Unfortunately Mr Clooney needed to lay off the cat food, he'd let himself go badly.

'What a lovely name for a cottage,' Katy said. 'What does it mean?'

Paige admitted with a giggle that the cottage had been called *Paige and Brian's* originally. After the divorce was finalised and she realised that she'd need the extra income, she came up with something that would work better for the tourists. She'd gone for the name of a Runrig song. It meant 'the morning light.'

It wasn't long before they were chatting away about anything and everything. Katy felt a fresh breeze sweeping into her life as she sat in Paige's small garden, the cats brushing against her legs while she sipped her first ever camomile tea. It tasted like piss, but she forced herself to drink it – she didn't want to offend her host.

Eventually Katy went up to her room. It had an ensuite, that was good. She'd be able to settle in overnight and stay self-contained. She was looking forward to the chance to shower properly after her night on the train. Paige had sternly told the cats to stay out of her room, which as every cat owner knows is all that's required when it comes to laying down the law to their pets. Katy couldn't resist the comedic value of a Facebook post announcing that Mr Pitt was in her bedroom and seemed to be none the worse for wear after his recent troubles in the Angelina camp.

Feeling fresh and invigorated after ten minutes under a power shower, she pulled on some fresh clothes and gave her knickers a rinse out in the basin. She reckoned there would be a lot of that in the weeks to come, she'd have to get used to it.

Paige was a thoughtful host. She'd placed a desk and chair at the bedroom window and a small armchair in the corner of the room. Katy sat in front of the window and contemplated her next move. Much as she wanted to explore Fort William, she didn't want to risk running into Olly. It was only a small town and the sort of place where a familiar face would stand out a mile.

Much as she hated having her movements dictated by a man again, she decided to give him some time to move on ahead of her. He'd proudly announced that he wouldn't be walking the official Great Glen Way, but would be loosely following the proper route and making several longer stop-offs along the way.

Katy decided to study the Polaroids while she had some time to kill. The sight of Spean Bridge flashing by on the train had whetted her appetite for the journey ahead. She pulled up her rucksack and felt in the pocket for the photos. The colour was terrible, faded and pallid, and she couldn't believe that they'd ever been so excited about the technology. Looking at them made her feel old. She was still slim, and even she thought that she was wearing okay, but there's nothing quite like the oblivious skinniness of youth. There was nothing on her in those days, and she'd always had great tits, even at nineteen.

And there was Emma. Her hair was longer now, and she'd actually improved with age. Elijah looked like the boy he was, but he'd felt like a man to her then, so mature and sure of himself. Nathan hadn't worn quite so well. She hadn't seen him for years, but his social media profiles depicted a man hurtling towards middle age and rapidly losing his hair. It was clear he had money though, as he always looked sharp and well-groomed. Life can be so cruel to guys, it's like Nick Kamen turning into Telly Savalas in front of your eyes.

It seemed like yesterday to Katy, and she felt herself

getting emotional about the lost time. What had she done with her life? Nothing. She'd studied and got a job. At best she'd occupied herself. Most of her youthful dreams had perished in that fire too.

Katy moved the image closer so that she could see it better. Isobel and Sarah's faces were a little blurred. She sifted through the photos for a sharper image. The door slammed downstairs as Paige returned from her expedition to buy cat food. She was chattering excitedly about something or other. Katy wondered if the cats had a clue what she was saying to them.

There was Isobel. Poor Izzy. Katy wondered if she was still so severe. Her drama degree had been her one shot at shaking off the shackles of her mother's strict Brethren upbringing, but after returning to help save the village shop, it had never come to anything career-wise. Katy examined the photo again. It looked like Isobel and Emma were holding hands – was she seeing that correctly? They were all of them very touchy-feely back then. She cringed as she recalled the group hugs and air kisses that accompanied their youthful exuberance.

Paige was heading up the stairs. Katy shuffled the pictures into a neat pile and placed them back in her bag. She took one out, the picture which had caused her to look twice, and quickly slid it into her wallet. That was another thing the blogs had suggested: no fussy purses for her while she was travelling on the road.

There was a cautious knock at the door.

'Come in!' said Katy, it's just me and Brad Pitt in here.'

She heard a little giggle.

'Can you get the door?' came Paige's voice. 'I've got my hands full.'

Katy darted towards the door handle, expecting Paige to

be carrying a tray, hopefully without a pot of camomile tea on it.

'You're a popular lady!' Paige said as Katy pulled the door open. 'I hope a bit of it rubs off on me.'

There was no tea tray. Instead, Paige was standing on the landing with a huge bunch of flowers.

'There's no name,' she said, obviously enjoying the mystery of it all. 'All the card says is *Have a safe journey.*'

CHAPTER FIVE

'Damn!' said Katy. 'What's wrong with these guys, can't they take no for an answer?'

'Oh, I'm sorry. Have I done something wrong?' asked Paige. Her face had changed from a bearer of good news to don't shoot the messenger.

'Sorry, it's not your fault. It's some guy I met on the train journey up here. How does he know I'm even here?'

Paige placed the flowers on a small table which was positioned on the landing outside Katy's room. She moved the empty vase that had been on it to the side.

'We won't be needing that then,' she said. 'Anything I can do to help?'

'It's a long story,' Katy said, preoccupied with how Olly might know her whereabouts. Had he looked in her bag? At her phone? 'Let's put it this way, I need to take much more care about the men I speak to. I'm seriously beginning to question my judgment.'

'Amen to that!' Paige replied, chancing a small smile to see if she could coax Katy out of her worries. 'My ex was okay for years. Well, he could be a bit of a prat and he did love a bit of mansplaining, but when he hit forty, something happened to him. He turned into a middle-aged old fart. He was always moaning. He drove me spare but he clearly appealed to someone, because he ran off with some young totty. Bastard!'

'They're not all the same,' Katy replied, in spite of her annoyance unwilling to tar an entire gender with the same brush. 'But some of them are idiots, you're right!'

'What you need is a night on the town. There's not much of a town, mind you, but a girl can get a good meal, a nice drink and a bit of live music. What do you say?'

Katy hadn't intended to eat out in restaurants, not wanting to blow her budget, but what the hell. How could one night out on the town hurt? And she liked Paige. They were completely different people, but she was nice – a bit whacky, but she'd be fun to go out with.

'Let's do it!' she said. 'Show me what Fort William has to offer. How about we head out for six? I can't be out too late, I have a 20km walk to do tomorrow, and we can't go anywhere too posh, I've only come prepared for hiking.'

'Don't worry,' Paige smiled. 'Anybody without a beard looks attractive in this place. Even better if you're a woman without a beard. You'll be fine, they're used to tourists.'

So that was that. They went their separate ways to get changed and reconvened at the front door at the appointed time. It wasn't long before Katy found herself sitting in a seafood restaurant admiring the views of the loch and squinting to see the Camusnagaul ferry across the water. For the first time since she'd left London she felt a sense of freedom and release. Louis was hundreds of miles away, and she had her whole life in front of her.

She watched Paige manoeuvre some revolting looking shellfish out of its black enclosure. Fortunately, it being Scotland, there was nothing too exotic on the menu. She played it safe and stayed with seared salmon. Paige looked as if she was preparing to ask something.

'I hope you don't mind me asking, but who sent you those flowers? They looked very nice, they'll have cost a bob or two.'

That had been troubling Katy too. They were expensive flowers. Olly was an internet entrepreneur – he could have been a millionaire as far as she knew. She'd seen enough rich people come into the accountancy firm looking as if they didn't have a penny to their name. However, he had opted for the cheap seats on the train. If he was loaded, surely he wouldn't have endured a night with his head dropping forward every five minutes and drool leaking from his mouth in public? But then, he hadn't. He'd found himself a bed for the night. Katy's. Had she been really stupid?

'I'm pretty sure it was this guy I met on the train. He helped chase my ex away before we left London. It's a long story.'

There was no way that Paige was going to leave a yarn like that untold. Before long they were sharing the details of their lives. It felt great to unload about Louis to someone who wasn't sick to death of hearing about the prick. And Paige had had her own share of misfortune. Her husband had run away with a twenty-three year old who worked at one of the bars in the town.

Katy could only imagine how much that would hurt. What did a middle-aged woman have to fight back with when there was some toned and beautifully waxed young woman on the scene? But Paige knew, and that's why she was living in the comfortable home they'd bought together and he was living in a crappy bedsit in the town centre. Paige hoped the perfectly threaded eyebrows and delightfully manicured bush were worth it.

As the plates were cleared and a second half-bottle of wine demolished, Paige suggested moving to one of the pubs to listen to ceilidh music. Katy knew she should refuse, but she'd had too much wine and her defences were low. She was in that delightful state of drunkenness where her inhibitions were fast disappearing but she wasn't yet destined to spend the next day with her head perched over the toilet. If she had a couple of soft drinks next, she reckoned she'd be fine.

Paige was a laugh when she got warmed up. They howled at her stories of a marriage going off the boil, even though they were laced with the sadness of a failed relationship. She told how he'd started behaving differently when he met his new woman – this was before Paige caught them in the marital bed and threw the bastard out.

He'd taken up cycling and shaved his legs for increased speed, only he'd made a mess of it and his skin ended up looking like a plucked chicken that had been dragged through a hedge. Paige also revealed how he'd started taking Viagra. Things had not been good in the bedroom for several months, but who was Paige to complain? She had her own struggles with hot flushes, and periods which went AWOL for months at a time. He'd decided to double-dose one evening and spent the entire night in the local hospital with priapism and an irregular heartbeat. It had terrified Paige who'd thought he was dying. When she realised that he wasn't taking the pills for her benefit, she wished he'd been stuck with that indestructible hard-on for the rest of his life. It would serve him right.

Katy kept it light. Paige's stories were funny, even

though she could tell that her new friend was desperately sad things had ended the way they had. She'd expected to spend the rest of her days with the grumpy old bastard, not find herself alone at her time of life. Katy glossed over Louis's violence, but it felt good to take the piss out of his intricate personal grooming regime. She enjoyed telling Paige about the time she put his expensive boxer shorts in the wash with her new red knickers and ruined £200 worth of designer underwear in one fell swoop. Laughing at him like that made her feel as if she was fighting back at last.

It was a great evening. The ceilidh band put her in the mood for a stay in Scotland. She'd always loved it up there, since the moment they'd first seen the mountains as they drove through Glencoe.

Then, out of nowhere, things took a sudden turn. Paige had popped off to the toilets and Katy was watching the band, wondering how many blankets could be knitted out of the facial hair sported by the musicians. They had some serious beards – she'd never seen anything like it.

Someone was moving towards the table. It's an occupational hazard, guys making a move on women when they're alone in bars. Only she knew this man already.

'Hi Katy,' he said. 'Fancy running into you here.'

It was Olly.

Katy was aware of the text arriving on her phone, but was more preoccupied with the man in front of her.

'Look, Olly, this is too much. You need to get lost, right now. Those flowers were plain creepy.'

'Hey, I was only saying hello. We're not teenagers. I don't have to ignore you.'

'After the way you've behaved, you're creeping me out. I want you to leave me alone. I'm grateful for your help on the train, and I enjoyed spending the night with you, but that's it. Okay? No relationship, no second night together. And no more flowers.'

'Whoa, hang on a minute. I didn't send you any flowers. We went our separate ways this morning, like you asked. Yes, I tried my luck again – what guy wouldn't? You're an attractive lady, and I had a great time with you. But I'm a big boy and I know how it works. You say no, I take it on the chin. But I didn't send you any flowers. In fact, I even changed my plans after what you said. I'm staying here for a few days because I wanted to give you a headstart. I'm no bloody weirdo.'

'So who sent them, Olly? Nobody knows I'm here except you. Did you look at my phone when you found it in the toilet? Are you following me?'

'Jesus, Katy. Do you know how crazy you sound right now? Come on, that man of yours has screwed you up. I was taking a shit this morning, okay, and I saw your phone when I was washing my hands. It had to be yours, it was your bling. I didn't look at your bloody phone. In any case, it'll have a password on it, won't it?'

Katy's face reddened. That was another thing Emma had warned her about, another security tip she'd ignored. 'You have fingerprint recognition on that thing, so why don't you use it?' Emma had scolded. She wished she had now, but all that password nonsense had seemed too much trouble. Besides, there was nothing on her phone that would be of any interest to anyone else. So no, it was not password protected. She wasn't going to admit that to Olly and changed the subject back to the flowers.

'Then you must be following me. There's no way

anybody else could have sent the flowers. How did you do it if you didn't look at my phone?'

Katy knew that she was sounding like a bunny boiler, but she was getting desperate – what with Louis at Euston, the mysterious letter in the post, and now the flowers. So what if she was being paranoid? She had good reason to be.

Paige came back from the toilets and was immediately alerted to the tension in the air.

'Everything alright here?' she asked, her eyes flitting between Olly and Katy. 'I know John the barman. If you need any help, just tell me.'

'It's fine, it's okay,' Olly said, looking hard at Katy. He hadn't put her down as a crazy. He was beginning to re-evaluate.

'Look Katy, I'm sorry you think I did something. You're a nice lady, a lot of fun. But you need to ditch this idea that I'm following you. I'm not. Fort William is a small town. This is the best place to go for a pint and some live music. It's no big deal that I ran into you here. It's coincidence, that's all. And I didn't send you those flowers.'

Olly walked away. Katy felt like crap. She wouldn't have put Olly down as that type of guy either, but she'd made mistakes before. Look how wrong she'd been about Louis. He had to have sent the flowers. She'd made the Airbnb switch at the last moment, and he was the only one who could have known. She wanted to scream. Paige saw her frustration.

'Let's move on and leave the tosser to his pint. There's a coffee bar which should still be open. We can get something to keep us awake and talk about it. How does that sound?'

Katy didn't particularly want to rake over the coals, but she did want to get out of that pub. All of a sudden the sound of a Scottish jig was annoying the hell out of her. She stood up to leave, scanning the room for Olly. He'd retreated into the crowd and was nowhere to be seen.

As it turned out, a coffee was what Katy needed. It knocked back the last remnants of alcohol that hadn't been diluted by the soft drinks and helped her to think clearly. As Paige waited at the counter for top-ups, she remembered the text that had come in while she was ranting at Olly. It was from Emma.

Hi hun, didn't want to ring you on your first day in Scotland, but I had a message on Facebook from Elijah's old tutor. He teaches in Dundee now and saw you were in Scotland. He asked if it's okay to contact you. I said I'd need to check. You okay with that? He wants to meet with you I think. Hope you're having fun! Em x

Katy considered phoning – she really wanted to hear Emma's voice. But Paige was heading back to the table and it would be antisocial. Instead, she texted back, brief and quick.

Sure, give him my mobile number x

'I got you some chocolate brownie. I know it's late, but what the hell! We deserve it.'

'Thanks, Paige. I'm sorry I've been such a pain in the arse. I hope all your guests aren't like me.'

'It's no trouble. I haven't had as much fun in a long time. I normally get hill walkers and wildlife lovers – you're different from my regular guests. I'm pleased I met you.'

'Paige, I want to show you something. It might seem weird, but I want to see what someone who wasn't around at the time makes of it.'

'Sure. Sounds interesting. What is it?'

Katy took the Polaroid out of her wallet. She showed it

to Paige and said nothing. Paige examined it, trying to work out what she was looking at.

'It's a photo of a bunch of kids,' she began. 'Has to be Scotland with that hill in the background. Is that right?'

Katy nodded.

'What do you see?'

Paige looked hard.

'Oh, that's you! Nice bloke, was he your boyfriend?'

'Yes.'

'You look like you're in love. And this girl looks head over heels too.'

'Who?' Katy asked, intrigued.

'Look, their hands are touching. Are they a couple?'

'That's Emma and Izzy,' Katy replied. 'So, I'm not imagining the hands then?'

'Difficult to tell,' Paige said, 'but yes, I'd say so.'

Katy had never seen it back then – it was only when she looked at that picture again after so many years. That expression on Izzy's face. She seemed to be besotted with Emma, while Emma looked as if she was more interested in whoever was taking the photo.

Her mobile phone sounded again: two texts, one from Emma and another from an unknown number. She read the text from Emma first.

Have passed on your number. His name is Roger Parry if you've forgotten. Says he'll be in touch. Ems x

Paige was still studying the photo, so Katy checked out the second text.

Hello Katy, thanks for letting me contact you. You may remember me from university, I was Eli's personal tutor. I saw on Facebook that you're in my neck of the woods. Would it be possible to meet up? Elijah shared a confidence with me many years ago and I kept it to myself. As I've got older, it feels like something that I should have shared with you after he died. Very keen to see you in person. Sorry, this must be a bit of a shock. I should have told you a long time ago. Hoping that you're well. Regards, Roger Parry.

Katy was stunned. The echoes of the past were roaring in her ears. For years they'd been whispers, but now their cry was persistent and demanding.

'Everything okay?' Paige asked.

'I've just heard from somebody I haven't even thought about for years. They're reconnecting because I'm in Scotland. It has to do with Elijah, the boy in that picture. It's so weird that he should contact me now.'

'That's social media for you,' Paige said, placing the photo on the table. 'I once discovered that I was on the same train as an old school friend because we both tweeted to moan about the delay to our journey at the same time. I messaged her: *That's not you, is it?* It was! We met up in her carriage and caught up on old times. Such an amazing coincidence.'

'If he's driving over from Dundee towards Spean Bridge, where's the best place to meet? It needs to be somewhere public.'

'Depends if you want scenery. There's parking at the Commando Memorial and it's on his route. Or if it's raining, there's always one of the bars in the village.'

'I remember that monument. It's not far from where we were staying. I'll meet him there – kill two birds with one stone. He might give me a lift into the village if I'm lucky. Okay if I text?'

Paige nodded and studied the photo again. Katy did a quick calculation about walking times and messaged Roger

Parry. The guidebook said it was a maximum five-hour walk from Fort William, and he'd have a three-hour drive from Dundee. She'd suggest two o'clock, but tell him to give her a window of half an hour in case she was held up. At least she wasn't hungover. She'd be on her way by nine o'clock prompt the next day.

The timing couldn't have been better. Whatever it was that Roger Parry had to say, she wanted to hear it. And she sure as anything was going to ask Emma about that photo. Secretive cow. Had she and Izzy had a thing going on that summer? Even after all those years, new questions were coming up.

But before she had a chance to hear what he wanted to say to her, Roger Parry would be dead.

Katy was proud of herself for getting up, breakfasted and out of Paige's house before nine o'clock. Truth be told, her mind had been active all night, turning over the events of the past few days. She'd been thinking about her dad too and wishing he was still around. She'd always felt safe with him there, and everything had been much simpler. Life seemed to be slipping away from her. She'd be middle-aged before she knew it.

Paige gave her a huge hug when she left, and Katy reciprocated. The two women had formed a strong bond in the short time they'd known each other.

'Remember, if you have any trouble give me a call. I'll be only too happy to come and help you out. I've loved having you here.'

Although Katy was walking the Great Glen Way, she

had no intention of sticking slavishly to it. She figured that she'd dip in and out as she pleased, and might even cheat and get the bus if it suited her. So long as she was in Inverness for the meet-up at the weekend, it didn't really matter. She also wanted to be as sure as she could that she wouldn't run into Olly again. He'd seemed earnest enough in the pub, but somebody must have sent those flowers.

For her first day of walking, Katy decided to stick to the official route. The timings were good. She'd skip Gairlochy, spend as long as she needed in Spean Bridge, and then make up any delay by bus, or even by hitching. It felt good to be weaving through the town centre and into the outskirts of Fort William, tracking the route of the canal along properly constructed paths, which gradually became rural tracks.

There was something about the landscape that connected with her. She loved it all. The air was so clean and fresh after all those years in the big smoke. As she walked along the pathway, occasionally passing a fellow traveller, for the first time in many months she felt strong. She was capable of being on her own. She didn't need anybody, and definitely not another idiot like Louis.

The websites she'd looked at had varied in their estimate of how long it would take her to get to Gairlochy, and after that there would be another hour's walk to the Commando Memorial, but she was pleased with the time she made. There were no blisters, no sprained ankles and only one visit to squat behind a bush for a pee. She'd have to get used to that. If some poor sod was unfortunate enough to be scanning the landscape with binoculars at the time, they'd be treated to a flash of her arse.

She thought about the letter. Who lived in Leytonstone? Who even had relatives in that area? And why the message now? Katy had no answers. She'd have to hope that whoever it was made themselves known to her. If they had some axe to grind, they wouldn't stay hidden for long.

At Gairlochy, Katy rejoined the road, walking towards Spean Bridge. She looked at her phone. She was making good time. Roger Parry had agreed to the meeting and told her not to rush, he'd wait if she was late. He'd offered to pick her up if she needed it, but Katy thought it best to stick to a landmark. She didn't know what the mobile phone signal would be like en route.

She hadn't been able to locate the place they'd stayed in that summer. She remembered the village, the Little Chef and the monument. They'd passed the monument to get to the wooden lodge, and she'd have to hope her memory would fill in the blanks. She had a couple of printouts of places that it might be. She'd ask in the village if she couldn't find it.

Just after one o'clock, her phone rang. It frightened the life out of her – she thought she was in a dead zone. It was Emma.

'Hi, I've got a free period. I thought I'd call.'

'Hi Ems, it's a really shitty signal out here, so don't be surprised if I disappear. I wish you could be here with me. Talk about a lot of memories!'

'I'll see you at the weekend. I'm looking forward to going up there again.'

'Hey, Ems, I've been having a good look at those old photos and it's got me thinking. You and Izzy ... I never noticed. You're not ... you're not gay, are you?'

'No, of course I'm not! You should know that of all people.'

'So what was going on with Izzy? I remember that big row you had. Did you have a lovers' tiff?'

It felt good to hear Emma's voice.

'No, nothing like that, not from my point of view anyway. You know what it was like when we were young. Elijah was the first bloke you ever slept with, you told me as much. I was going through an experimental phase at the time ...'

The call was breaking up. Katy moved to the side, trying to find the position that she'd been in originally.

'Say that again. The phone signal is crap.'

'I said that it was only a fling for me, a bit of fun. There was a teacher at secondary school who'd got me into Spare Rib magazine. It was feminism and all that. I wanted to give it a try. It was a phase, nothing serious. I've never done anything like it since. Well once. That threesome I told you about, remember? But it's not really my thing.'

'What about Izzy? I'd never noticed how she's looking at you in this picture – too young and stupid to see it, I suppose.'

'Well, you must know Izzy's gay. Didn't you ever figure that one out?'

'Really?' Katy asked, genuinely taken by surprise.

'Yes, but she would never have admitted it back then. She's more open about it now. Bloody religious upbringing and all that. Don't you remember how repressed she used to be? She hated herself for it. She thought she was unnatural in some way. It was just a bit of fun—'

The phone signal broke up and Katy only caught the beginning of the sentence. She'd fill in the gaps herself. She needed to cut this call short – she didn't want to miss Roger Parry.

'What was that row about? The moped incident, where

you had to come home in the car with us, and Izzy sat there scowling all night.'

'I'd broken it off with her. Remember we were sharing that bedroom? It had been an occasional thing at uni, but Izzy started getting all heavy about it when we were staying in the lodge. While we were waiting for you lot to arrive at Eilean Donan, I told her that after the holiday I wanted to finish it. I preferred guys. I wasn't nasty or anything, but it wasn't what I wanted any more. I said we could carry it on until the holiday finished.'

'Why didn't I know any of this? How could I have missed it?' Katy asked.

'You were besotted with Elijah. It was Elijah-this, Elijah-that, and you didn't give a shit about anybody else. You and I didn't become close until after his death. You're looking at it through adult eyes. It was different back then, we were so young, and anyhow, Izzy made me swear that I'd keep it a secret.'

'What did she say?' Katy asked. 'What did Izzy say when you told her it was over? She had a face like thunder when we got to the castle. I can still remember it now.'

'She was really pissed with me. She'd thought it was for real. She made me swear I wouldn't tell anybody, and I suppose I was a bit embarrassed about it myself. After Elijah died, well, it didn't seem important anymore.'

'How could Izzy have kept that from us for so long? I knew her mum was a strict old cow, but I didn't realise she was gay. I assumed she wasn't interested. Jesus, I was so self-absorbed.'

'She hated me for it,' Emma picked up, as the mobile phones continued their struggle to stay connected. 'She was so angry. It seemed funny when she stormed off on that moped of hers, but it hurt her badly. I was too young and stupid to see it at the time. We were in the middle of the row when you lot arrived in the car. I'll always remember what she said to me that day, the day of the fire. As she went roaring off into the distance on that bloody machine of hers, she almost spat the words into my face.

'She said to me, "I hope you and the rest of them burn in hell!"'

CHAPTER SIX

Katy was so preoccupied with what Emma had told her that she barely registered the scenery as she neared the monument. She'd cut the call short, worried that she might get distracted and miss her appointment.

She couldn't really remember Roger Parry. She hadn't had anything to do with him directly, but he was Elijah's personal tutor and they'd bump into him every now and then on campus. He seemed a bit pompous and full of his own self-importance, but that was only Katy's perception based upon a few casual encounters. Elijah seemed to get on well enough with him and as their relationship developed over that first academic year she began to understand how much of a sounding board Parry had been for her boyfriend.

She learned that Elijah had struggled to adjust to university life. Katy didn't know him then – they'd met towards the end of their first term. He had been bullied and had moved into a different hall of residence. He never told Katy the precise details because he was ashamed of admitting to being bullied as an adult, but it was always something that had lurked in the background. Katy didn't push it. The incident was over, the idiot who was responsible had been asked to leave the university due to a breach of his behaviour contract and that was that. Elijah moved into their accommodation block, and Katy met him in the laundry room one evening over a bag filled with dirty washing. He was having an asthma attack and she'd helped him through it by retrieving his inhaler from his room. And that was that, they hit it off immediately.

For Elijah, Roger had been a trusted confidant who had helped him to navigate a difficult time in his life. As somebody who had adeptly steered around the perils of the secondary school bully, it was a complete shock to become a victim in an adult and academic environment. It was, quite simply, the last thing he would have ever expected.

As the monument appeared in the distance, Katy tried to dismiss thoughts of the past and focus on the target ahead, but the stirring sight of the three commando figures looking across the stunning open landscape brought the summer of 1999 back with great clarity.

She was surprised at how quiet it was for the time of year. Every now and then a car would draw up, a couple would leap out, walk around the statue and take a selfie or two. They'd head over to the garden of remembrance, look around awkwardly as if they felt guilty about leaving such an important spot so soon, then drive off. There was no sign of Roger Parry, so Katy perched on the steps in front of the monument and checked her phone. No messages. And a weak signal.

It wasn't quite two o' clock. She was early and she was tired now too. Maybe she'd been optimistic to think that she could complete the entire Great Glen Way from a standing start with no preparation. She had all the time in the world.

She'd take a bus and skip a day's walking if she needed to. There was nothing to prove to anybody and, besides, now she had arrived she was minded not to move on as quickly as she'd planned. There were a lot of memories in this place, and she wanted to walk among them a while longer.

She'd booked into a B&B in the village for the night and was due in Laggan at the end of the next day. She decided there and then that she'd cancel Laggan, stay an extra night in Spean Bridge and take a bus to Fort Augustus. She felt a rush of exhilaration realising that this was her life now, she could make it up as she went along. After working in the city for so long, her life set by the comings and goings of the underground trains, it came as a blessed relief. It was an amazing feeling.

A car pulled up in the car park. Surely Roger Parry would come up to the monument and see her, he wouldn't just sit in his car? She thought back to how he'd looked in 1999. He had a good head of hair back then, and much of it was grey. It was difficult to age him. When you're eighteen, everybody seems ancient to you. He must have been late thirties, early forties, she thought, so he'd be in his sixties now. He might be retired. With men it was difficult. If he'd lost his hair, he'd be almost impossible to pick out in a crowd.

Katy looked hopefully at the red Fiat, but it wasn't long before an elderly couple got out and released two enthusiastic Scotties from the boot. They began their circuit of the monument. She was beginning to get fidgety. It was well past two o'clock now and she'd expected him to have got there early. It was Parry who'd asked for the meeting, not her. Maybe he'd got caught in traffic.

Katy needed to pee. In London you were never more than two minutes away from a Costa, Starbucks or McDonald's. In Scotland, gorse bushes were quickly becoming her best friend. When Roger arrived she decided to suggest driving into the village. She could use the facilities in a pub or tearoom.

Restless now, she stood up and scanned the area. The straps of her rucksack were rubbing her shoulders and she decided it would be safe to leave it on the steps. There were a couple of Japanese students taking pictures and the older couple were dawdling over from the memorial garden. It didn't look like a high-crime area.

As Katy walked over to the car park, she saw two cars that she'd missed, concealed from view by the banking. She stood at the top of the grassy area scanning them for signs of life. If Roger Parry was in one of them, he'd have to be blind to miss her.

She checked her phone. Messages and texts tended to get through even if the phone signal was bad. Nothing. He was more than twenty minutes late. Katy had to pee. If he didn't show up soon she'd have to find some cover further along the road. She dialled Roger's number. It rang and rang. Somewhere in the distance she could hear another phone ringing. When she ended the call, the echoing ring ended.

Katy scanned the roads which came to a fork beyond the Commando Monument. There were plenty of trees across the road and to the side. If things became critical, she could be relieving herself behind a bush within five minutes. The Japanese students climbed into their car and drove off, while the couple with the dogs looked at the statue and admired the scenery.

Katy decided to phone again. As the dial tone sounded in her ear, once again there was an echo from the car park. She gazed at the cars. There was a sleek black vehicle parked in the corner. She hadn't picked it out when she first surveyed the area, but it was out of place, too expensive to be seen somewhere like that. It had tinted windows which looked completely black from where she was standing.

She looked at the other cars. They were all empty. A bus swung into the car park and she ducked out of the way to let it pass. It was full of tourists – she ought to retrieve her rucksack before they started their tour of the monument. As they filed out of the bus, Katy checked the three approach roads for a final time. Damn Roger Parry, bloody lecturers always worked to their own timetable.

The call connected. She was standing directly in front of the black car this time and there was no doubt about it, the ringing was coming from inside. Katy stepped right up to the vehicle, moving her face up to the glass. It was impossible to see into the darn thing. She knocked on the driver's side window. Still no response. The phone continued to ring.

Gingerly she put her hand on the door handle.

'I'm going to open the door now to make sure you're okay. If you're in there, please give me a shout.'

The door clicked open. Katy waited for a response, half-expecting to find somebody in there sleeping. As she opened it fully, she saw the phone on the passenger seat. It took her a moment to take in the rest of the scene.

Roger Parry was in the driver's seat and at first she thought he was asleep. It looked as if he'd nodded off, his head tilted forward. But as she touched him on the shoulder, she realised in horror what she was looking at.

Roger Parry was dead. A leather belt was fastened tightly around his neck, looped round the headrest. He'd been strangled in his seat. Katy ended her call. The phone in the passenger seat went silent.

'Oh fuck! Hey, over here! I need some help over here!'

Katy instinctively pulled back from the car. She was waving frantically towards the group of tourists, while at the same time using her other hand to dial 999. She had to call the police. Roger's face showed signs of the struggle that must have taken place in that car. His seatbelt had kept him restrained, while the tightened belt around his neck had deprived him of oxygen. How different to her dad he looked in death. Terry had appeared at peace, as the sympathy cards suggested.

Katy felt strangely calm. She knew exactly what to do. Call the police, get some help and go for a piss. In that order. She'd need an empty bladder for when the police arrived.

'Jesus!' she gasped. His dick was partially out and it was his own belt that had been removed for the strangulation. What the hell had Roger Parry been up to? She wondered if this was some erotic asphyxiation thing. Maybe that's what the tinted glass was for. Seeing the older couple approach with the Scotties, she pushed the car door so that it was almost closed.

'You alright, luv?' the man said. One of the Scotties sniffed around her feet.

'There's been an accident,' Katy said. 'A man is dead inside this car.'

The woman stopped smiling. She stooped to pick up one of the dogs.

'Have you called the police?'

'Just about to,' Katy said. 'Can you keep an eye on the car? Don't touch anything as the cops will want to be all over it. And don't look inside either. It's not a pretty sight.'

'You're sure he's dead?' the man asked.

Katy nodded, and stepped away as the 999 call connected. The older couple moved to stand in front of the vehicle as if they were guarding it. The man picked up the second dog, realising the importance of leaving the immediate area as uncontaminated as possible. Katy figured they were more Miss Marple than CSI. They'd probably think the vicar did it.

Katy gave the details to the police, finished the call and rushed off across the road to pee. By that stage she didn't really care if everybody knew that she'd been to answer nature's call in the bushes.

By the time she returned, a large group of tourists from the coach had gathered round, sensing that something interesting was afoot. By the time Police Scotland arrived, it resembled a crime-scene Q&A session. They cleared the immediate area and set about taking control of the situation. Not long after, another car arrived.

As the person who'd discovered the body, Katy was taken to one side. The elderly couple had to hang about too. Everybody else was asked to leave contact details as well as hotel and travel information before they were ushered off the scene. It was a slick, well-oiled operation. It reminded Katy of 1999 – this was what had happened then.

She recognised the copper who was speaking to her. He'd been there all those years back, at the fire.

'You're not Alan Buchanan, are you?' she asked.

'Yes, and how would you know that?' he replied, studying her face.

'I'm Katy, Katy Wild. You'll remember who I am when I tell you I was there on the night of the fire in 1999. You were first on the scene. I can't believe you're still working for the police.'

'I remember that night and I suppose I remember you. It's so long ago now. Katy Wild was the young girl who lost her boyfriend ... was that really you?'

Katy nodded. She was amazed she remembered his name, but being in that area it was all coming back to her: PC Alan Buchanan, an Englishman working in Scotland. He'd stood out on that night because of his accent. She remembered him because he'd let her cry on his shoulder. Everybody else was asking questions, questions and more questions. He'd shown some compassion. She'd liked him.

'You seem to have a habit of showing up when there's trouble,' he said, not thinking. 'I'm sorry, I shouldn't have said that. But you must admit, it's a bit of a coincidence. Nothing ever happens around here, only the occasional drugs bust or car crash. That fire was the biggest event of my policing career. And now, almost at retirement, this happens. Do you want to tell me all about it?'

Katy gave him an exact account of everything that had happened. She had nothing to hide. She showed him her phone records, explained how Roger Parry's contact had come out of the blue, and walked him through every step of how she'd discovered the body. He'd been promoted since they last met and he was now DS Buchanan.

'We'll need to take your fingerprints,' he said as he finished making notes. 'It looks like he was into deviant sexual practices, but we'll have to investigate fully. Can I take your contact details in case we have any questions? Where are you staying tonight?'

Katy gave him the name of the B&B that she'd booked. It suddenly occurred to her that this might make it difficult to leave the country. There'd be a fatal accident inquiry and she'd need to give evidence. That was all she needed, a complication in her new, carefree life. Couldn't Roger Parry have waited to beat himself off until after they'd spoken? She'd never know what he wanted to tell her now.

The area was crawling with police officers and forensics staff. The monument was closed off and some poor constable had been assigned the task of turning frustrated tourists away.

'Do you want me to run you down to the B&B? I know Judd and Ruby, and they'll no doubt want to hear all the gossip.'

Katy was delighted to receive the offer. Her legs had stiffened and the thought of having to walk the eight miles to the village was no longer an attractive prospect.

'Where were we staying when we came here?' Katy asked. 'It can't have been far away.'

'It wasn't,' DS Buchanan replied as he buckled his seat-belt. 'You were a couple of miles down that road. The land has been sold a few times now, and nobody has done anything with it. When you visit it you'll see the skeleton of a building that was being put up on the site but never finished. It's a shame, it was a lovely location for a house.'

Katy looked along the road. It was going to be a pain in the arse having to walk everywhere. She wished she'd thought things through a little more carefully. They drove into the village in silence. Katy couldn't really remember it.

'Here we are, the Highland Heather B&B. You'll like Judd and Ruby, they do a great Scottish breakfast. I'll come and see you again tomorrow. We'll give things some time to calm down a bit up at the monument, but I'm sure there'll be more questions to ask.'

'That's great, thank you. I really appreciate this. I'm exhausted – I only want to sleep.'

Judd and Ruby were very nice people, but their over-attentiveness was exactly what Katy didn't need at that moment. She craved an anonymous city hotel where she'd be thrown a keycard and left to her own devices. Judd and Ruby insisted on knowing everything that had happened up at the monument, where she came from and where she was going. When they finally showed Katy her room, every detail of its facilities was itemised one-by-one.

She dared not mention that she'd been to Spean Bridge before. All she wanted to do was to remove her boots, flop on her bed, and go to sleep. Her brain was fried with everything that had happened that afternoon and her body exhausted from the long walk. At last the doorbell buzzed downstairs and Judd and Ruby left her on her own to go and harass some other poor guest.

Katy didn't know how long she slept, but she was out from the moment she heard the door of her room click shut. It was dark when she awoke. Something had disturbed her. What was it? She fumbled for the lamp at the side of the bed and found the switch. She looked around. The noise wasn't her phone. There had been another sound which had aroused her from her slumber.

Her eyes were drawn by the sound of footsteps in the corridor outside. There was something on the floor. Somebody had slipped an envelope through the gap under the door.

Katy had been antsy all night and awoke far too early the next morning. She was dying to know what Alan Buchanan had to tell her. He'd scribbled a note on B&B stationery, deciding not to wake her up to tell her his news. They'd found something in the car and needed to talk to her about it. She wished he'd just stormed into her room and woken her up. Now she had to wait until he arrived at nine o'clock.

Katy heard movement downstairs a little after seven. By that time she'd showered, dried her hair, put on clean clothes and read every new Facebook post that she could lay her hands on. She was starving too, having missed dinner the night before.

B&B wasn't her normal style. She'd already had to rinse some guy's shaving debris from around the basin in the shared bathroom – and open the window to give it an airing. She didn't want to touch the sides of the shower for fear of some hairy male body having brushed against the glass before her.

Breakfast was as bad. She'd hoped to put away a plate of bacon and eggs and then enjoy a second cup of tea over a morning newspaper. Instead, the dining room was so small she had to shuffle up and share a table with five middle-aged men on a walking holiday, all talking and laughing loudly. To make matters worse, the bacon was fried, not grilled. That was it, no more B&Bs.

Eventually, the men moved away, leaving her on her own at a table that looked as if it had been hit by a whirlwind. There was one other couple sitting at the second table, talking in bored, stilted sentences.

'Isn't that garden lovely? It's been beautifully planted.'

'I love the plates they've used to line the walls. Is that bone china?'

Relief in the form of DS Buchanan finally arrived. Judd got him a coffee and hovered a little too long as he cleared the table around them.

'What do you want to talk to me about?' Katy asked.

'You were fast asleep when I called last night, and I thought it better to let you get a good night's rest. We need to get your fingerprints as soon as we can so that we can eliminate your tracks from the crime scene—'

'You're calling it a crime scene?' Katy asked.

He was caught off-guard by that.

'Well no, not a crime scene. Let's just say the scene of the incident, shall we?'

'It was an accident, wasn't it? That's what it looked like.'

'I can't say until the investigation is completed, but I do need to ask you about this.'

DS Buchanan reached into a large brown envelope and took out a couple of scanned pages. They were printouts that had been taken from a notebook of some sort.

'What's this?' Katy asked, taking the papers as he handed them over to her.

'We're not sure. We thought you might be able to help. A hardback notebook was found underneath the passenger seat concealed inside an AA map book. It looks like whatever he wanted to say to you was contained in that notebook. It's marked confidential and it looks quite old, you can see that from the dates inside: 1997 to 1999. It looks like some sort of note-taking from sessions with students.'

'Why are you showing me?' Katy asked, scanning the handwritten text in the images.

'Elijah's name is in there. That was the name of your friend, wasn't it? Elijah? Well, look at the entries from 1998 and 1999. That's your boyfriend, isn't it?'

Katy skimmed the text. She got the gist very quickly.

'This is incredible,' she said. 'These must be Parry's notes from his private sessions with students. Elijah was being bullied in 1998 in our first term. That's what these notes are about. And Nathan's name is in here too. Did you know that he was with us when the lodge burned down?'

'I hadn't made that connection. That's very interesting.'

DS Buchanan made a note in a small jotter taken from his pocket.

'Do you think he wanted to talk to me about something in this diary?'

'I think that we need to drive to the station to get your fingerprints taken and sort out anything else required by the investigating team,' he replied, a little too cryptically for Katy's liking.

The last time they'd spoken, in 1999, she was barely an adult. The police presence after the fire had terrified her. She was older and wiser now and she wasn't taking any shit. She was used to dealing with clients who were withholding details of their income. She was skilled at sniffing out their deceptions and challenging those who didn't want to come clean with the Inland Revenue.

'You know that I'm nothing to do with this, don't you?' Katy asked directly. 'The car was in the middle of the car park, and there was a busload of tourists there. You've got my phone call to Emma and my calls to Roger confirm my story.'

'You're not under suspicion. We know it's nothing to do with you. It looks like he was jerking himself off in the car and trying to give himself some sort of sexual thrill. Only ...'

'Only what?'

'This notebook that we found has messed things up a bit. It looked like a straightforward case of man jerks off in car and gets more than he bargained for. But there are some entries in there that bring up something that happened when the lodge burned down. It's something to do with your friend Nathan.'

'Is it in these papers?' Katy asked, shuffling through them and scanning for Nathan's name. She couldn't see anything, only passing references to how Elijah's best friend was Nathan and how Nathan had helped him through the bullying. There was even mention of how Nathan had stood up for him once, getting a bloodied nose in the process. She hadn't known that. It was interesting, but hardly a major revelation.

'Come on, DS Buchanan. If it's connected with what happened at the lodge, you'll need to tell me sooner or later. What is it?'

'I'm sorry to bring all this back up again after so many years, but I guess that's why you're here, isn't it? You're revisiting the past, trying to go over what happened.'

Now it was his turn to hit a bullseye.

'You're absolutely right. I haven't been back since it happened. I could never face it. I need to confront that past. I want to understand it better. I was hoping that Roger Parry was going to help me, but it turns out he couldn't keep his flies up. If there's something in that diary that can help me get a better understanding of what happened, don't I have a right to know?'

DS Buchanan nodded.

'You're right. You do. To be honest with you that night's troubled me all of my policing career. You youngsters ... well, it was a complete mess.'

'But it was an accident, right? That was the official verdict: accidental death.'

'It was,' Buchanan said, seeming to Katy a little weary now, 'but this diary has introduced something that never came up in the interviews afterwards. Nobody mentioned it. I know, I read the transcripts. We don't have many cases like that in this area. Being involved in that case is what made me become a detective.'

'So, if you'll forgive my language, what the fuck has

changed things all of a sudden? What's got your police antennae twitching?'

'Well, don't shoot the messenger,' Buchanan said, hoping she was up to receiving this bit of news.

'Just say it!' Katy said, exasperated at his prevarication.

'You know that boyfriend of yours – Elijah? There's no easy way of saying this. I think he might have been having a relationship with your friend Nathan.'

CHAPTER SEVEN

Katy barely registered the fingerprinting and DNA swab. She was too preoccupied with what Buchanan had told her about Nathan. The investigative team were telling her they needed to check her phone records and they wanted her laptop too, but it was just a stream of babble to her.

If she clocked anything, it was how much the procedure had changed since she was nineteen. It was a well-oiled machine of evidence collection and protection. These people knew their job and they did it well. She was blameless in Roger Parry's death so had nothing to worry about, but being without her phone and laptop was going to be a pain. The police wanted to hang onto them, and that was fair enough, but she needed to carry a phone with her. She'd been a teenager when Suzy Lamplugh had disappeared, and her parents had drummed into her the importance of letting somebody know your whereabouts. In this case, with no surviving parents, Emma had copped for that job.

Buchanan told her he had an old Nokia at home he was happy for her to take if it still charged. It wasn't as if the

Great Glen Way was the most hazardous place on earth, but he understood the importance of Katy having a phone.

She signed the inevitable paperwork and he walked her through to the small staff area.

'Tea? Coffee?'

'Yes, tea, lovely. Thank you. You won't forget that phone, will you? I only booked at Judd and Ruby's for one night. I need to rearrange my accommodation plans now and I'm going to need it.'

'I tell you what, we'll pick it up when I run you back to Spean Bridge. I live on the outskirts of Fort William and it's an easy diversion. It's pretty basic by today's standards, but the battery lasts for days – weeks actually. It's indestructible too!'

He smiled at her. Katy reckoned he must be almost sixty. When they'd last met, he must have been not much older that she was now. He'd seemed so mature and in command at the time of the fire, but now she was at the same age she still didn't feel like that inside. She wondered what kind of a life he'd had, stuck up there in the Highlands. Was she the proverbial bad penny, turning up once again on his patch? She'd been involved in the two most important events of his career.

The tea arrived. She was ready for it – the mouth swab had been simple enough, but she wanted to wash the experience away.

'I'll get you those photocopies.'

Katy nodded. As he left the room, she took a sip of tea. The mugs were from some local insurance company which was based in the town, and one of them was chipped.

She instinctively reached into her pocket for her mobile phone. It wasn't there of course. Another bad habit, punctuating moments of silence with a glance at your phone. She felt naked without it.

Buchanan returned, clutching a pile of papers. He placed them in front of her.

'I'm letting you see these because I'm as certain as I can be from your statement that you were the intended recipient. Whatever he was coming to talk to you about was related to these documents. These are copies, but I was looking for mentions of your friends, and it seems to be the best place to start. Can you give them a look over? See what you think.'

Katy was eager to read this information. Elijah was long dead. She thought that confidentiality probably didn't count after death. Besides, Parry had wanted her to see something in there, and she had to figure out what it was.

Buchanan had been thorough, he knew his data protection law. He'd only given her access to the handwritten passages which related to Elijah. There were no other personal details in there. It would have been meaningless to her anyway, as the chances of her recognising any of the other students were slim.

She scanned the text. She was shocked to read details of the bullying Elijah had encountered. It had been psychological and, at times, physical. She wondered how Roger Parry could have listened to Elijah telling him all of that and not taken any action. She supposed his role as counsellor was to listen and guide, to honour the wishes of the student. She'd never known how much the bullying had affected Elijah. She felt cross with herself for asking so few questions about it when he'd attempted to confide in her.

She read on and saw her own name. Elijah had moved accommodation blocks after Parry had talked him into taking action over the bullying. There he'd met Katy, and she was pleased to see how she'd entered Parry's notes like a breath of fresh air. There was nothing personal in there, only observations and comments which reflected Elijah's changed circumstances.

10/11 E has met a female student in new hall. Very excited and hoping to get to know her better. Very positive and optimistic, complete change from previous month. Seems much happier in himself.

27/11 E now started dating K. Completely changed his outlook. Met them in corridor earlier this week, clearly very happy in each other's company. Great to see.

Katy felt her eyes tearing up. Reading these notes had taken her back to a more innocent time and place. Her mum and dad were alive, she was in love, they had everything ahead of them.

'I'm sorry if it's difficult reading,' Buchanan said, taking his first sip of now cooled tea.

Katy continued reading. Her eye caught Nathan's name. This is what she wanted to read. This was new information to her.

12/2 E concerned about friend, Nathan. Said Nathan was good friend, but intense. Both parents died shortly before starting uni. No problem for E until he and K started dating. Has pushed N out of the picture and he doesn't appear to be taking it well. E doesn't want to spoil friendship, but needs space. Advised to give it some time.

4/3 E still concerned about N. Things going well with K, bullying seems to have been put behind him. N very moody and intense. Is N gay? Didn't mention to E, but seems possible. Jealousy perhaps? E definitely not gay? Action: N is computing student. Speak to Prof. Maxwell. N okay?

Katy thought back to uni. This was crazy. Nathan had

married Sarah and they'd been together for years. He couldn't be gay. They'd hooked up immediately after Elijah's death, thrown together by tragedy, she'd thought. Sarah had always made her intentions clear, although it had taken a life-changing incident like the fire to shake Nathan out of whatever was holding him back.

For Katy, Nathan had just been somebody who came with Elijah. They hadn't been friends before – Nathan was doing a computing course and there was no reason for her to have met him. But now she thought about it, he was around a lot. On nights when they went out as a couple, Elijah would always want to get out of halls promptly to make sure that nobody tagged along. Had that been all about Nathan?

It was too long ago to remember. He had some important job in tech now, and he always seemed to be away from home. They'd all known that his parents had died, but he'd never spoken about it. She couldn't even remember where the information had come from. Apparently they had died in a car crash two months before he started at uni. She was aware that the staff seemed to keep an eye out for him in their first year, but only in terms of him having regular meet-ups with his tutor, Professor Maxwell. That hadn't seemed unusual at the time.

Katy scanned the notes to the end of that academic year. There was nothing she didn't know already. They mentioned Elijah's concerns about the year one exams and about his holiday plans too. Regular student stuff, nothing more about Nathan.

'What do you think? Could Nathan have been having a relationship with Elijah?' Buchanan asked.

'I can see why you thought that might be the case, but I don't think there's anything there. Nathan's married. He has been for years. Elijah never said anything to me about it.'

'You see a lot of things in my job, even in a rural place like this. You learn a lot about people. It sounds like a serious case of jealousy to me. Believe me, I've seen it all. If it can happen, it will happen.'

'I still think you're barking up the wrong tree,' Katy replied. 'And whatever it was, it blew over. I don't know why Roger Parry was coming to speak to me. I can't see anything particularly revealing in his notes. Are you sure you got all of it?'

'Yes, I'm certain it's all there. We might as well head back. If you want to use the ladies' room before we go, I'll drop these papers into my office and we can meet back in the staffroom.'

He walked with her into the corridor and pointed to the end of the hallway.

'Don't go wandering off please.'

The toilets were basic and functional, no place to hang around. Once again, Katy fumbled for her phone. She cursed when she realised it wasn't there. She wanted to catch up with Emma. She washed her hands, checked her hair and headed back into the corridor. She caught sight of somebody coming out of the gents toilet to her right and did a double-take. There was something familiar about his shape and the way he moved. She knew this person.

She turned around. She'd been right. What had she been thinking about bad pennies? Here was another one.

It was Olly. He was standing there, smiling at her.

———

'Fucking hell, Olly! Haven't you pissed off yet?'

He turned to face her. He was cross now, she could see that much.

'Screw you, Katy. I'm going about my business and you keep turning up out of nowhere. I thought you'd be halfway along the Great Glen Way by now. I gave you enough of a head start for Christ's sake. I wish I'd left you to sort out your own bloody boyfriend on that train. I'm beginning to wonder if he'd been driven to it—'

Olly stopped dead and his expression changed.

'I'm really sorry, Katy. I didn't mean that. That was a shitty thing to say, but you seem to think I'm the enemy. I'm here because my laptop got stolen in the pub that night I saw you. That's all. It's complete coincidence. Fort William is a small place. I'm not following you.'

'Is everything alright out here?'

It was Buchanan. His finely tuned hearing had sensed a conflict along the corridor.

'It's fine,' Katy said. 'It was my fault. I jumped the gun. I'm sorry... I apologise, Olly.'

'Okay, thanks. I appreciate it. Enjoy your walking, Katy.'

He crossed the corridor to one of the interview rooms. A police officer had come out to see what was going on. They had a sixth sense for this stuff, the cops.

Katy and Buchanan headed the opposite way towards the reception area.

'You know that guy?' Buchanan asked when he was certain they wouldn't be overheard.

'A little,' Katy answered. She could feel her face reddening again. 'Why?'

'It's nothing really, but he had his phone and laptop stolen. We get a bit of that in Fort William – they usually turn up for sale the same day in one of the local pubs, but his stuff has gone completely AWOL. It's unusual.'

'What do you know about him?' Katy asked.

'Not much. Seems like a nice guy. It happens a lot. Someone plans to go walking in the area and is pissed off because he's lost his tech. Which reminds me, we need to get that phone for you.'

Katy was shaken by Olly's reappearance, but every time she replayed the scenario in her head, he came out clean. It was Louis. He'd screwed her up. Not every man was a bastard.

She was thankful that Buchanan changed the subject by the time they were in the car. They picked up the Nokia from his house. He still had the charger and there was just over a pound of credit left on it. It would do for emergencies until the police let her have hers back, and if she didn't get it back she'd get a replacement in Inverness. She was due an upgrade anyway.

Buchanan was one of the good guys. He kissed his wife at the front door before returning to the car with the phone. She gave Katy a friendly wave. Some people made things look so easy. Marriage, work, life ... Buchanan seemed to have it all. Soon he'd be retired on a police pension, away from all the nonsense of the workplace. Lucky bugger, he deserved it.

'I'll run you up to where the lodge was if you want?' he volunteered as they drove off. His wife stayed waving from the door until they were out of sight.

'Can you point out where it is? I need to sort out a place to stay, so I won't go there now. When am I okay to move on?'

'You're not a suspect, so you're free to leave any time you want. We've got your contact details. You're in the area for another week or thereabouts?'

Katy nodded.

'Yes, I'm flying out to Spain after I've met up with my

friends in Inverness, but that's still Europe. You'll be able to get hold of me easily enough,' she said with a smile.

Buchanan's phone rang. He checked his rear-view mirror and pulled onto the verge.

'Buchanan. Yes ... right ... okay ... Yes, she's with me now. Okay to mention it? Right. See you later.'

'What is it?'

'There's been a development in the case.'

They were passing the Commando Monument. Part of the car park was still cordoned off, and a lone police officer was standing next to the tape. The tourists had returned and Parry's car had gone. Everything would soon be back to normal, as if nothing had happened. Buchanan surveyed the area as they drove by and soon swung a left turn.

'They think Parry was murdered,' he said as they began to drive along the much narrower road. 'The belt was in the wrong position. The buckle was at the back. It had been pulled from behind. If he'd been jerking off in there, it would have been at the front where he could tighten it himself. You didn't move anything, did you?'

Katy didn't speak for a moment. Everything had seemed okay when she thought he'd been up to some kind of sex game. To think that he might have been killed was shocking.

'I touched him and moved the seatbelt, but there was no way his belt could have worked its way round his neck from that. It honestly didn't occur to me to look at the way it had been buckled.'

'You're not under any suspicion, Katy. The forensics guys will eliminate your DNA. It might be some sex game gone wrong. Maybe somebody did a runner – they might have panicked. Who knows?'

He pulled in at the start of a forest track bounded by trees.

'Here it is.'

'Do you want me to drive you up there? I'm happy to ... if you want?'

Katy looked around her. It was just as she remembered: a narrow track disappearing through the trees, barely suitable for driving. This is where life had taken its sudden turn all those years ago.

She checked the dashboard and saw it was after two o'clock.

'Thanks, I know where it is now. I'd never have found it on my own. But we need to move on and get back to Judd and Ruby's to see if I can get a bed for the night.'

It was bad news at the B&B. They were fully booked. They'd had to clear Katy's room and get it cleaned for the next guests.

'Can I use the phone?' Katy asked.

'Of course you can. No charge. Use it as much as you like.'

Ruby was doing her best to solve the situation, while Judd was more interested in nattering to one of his mates in the small bar area.

'I might be able to help,' she said. 'You keep using the main phone and I'll give my friend a call on my mobile.'

Katy felt hopeful. It was a tourist area, somebody would be able to put her up for the night. Buchanan was hovering in the lobby. He felt responsible for making sure she was okay.

'I'm fine,' Katy said. 'I'll find somewhere. You've got the Nokia number. I'll text you to let you know where I'm staying. That old thing does text, doesn't it?'

'Who are you calling an old thing?' he smiled. 'Yes, it does text. I've put my mobile number into the address book for you and you've got my card as well, so you know where to find me.'

Katy called Emma who didn't answer – school was still on. She left a message.

'Hell, Ems, you won't believe what happened after we spoke yesterday. Can you give me a call? I can't call you, I haven't any credit. Check your caller ID for my number. I've got a new phone. Don't ask!'

Not the most coherent update that she'd ever left, but it would have to do. Besides, Ruby was back and it looked like she'd got good news.

'I've got you a place to stay,' she beamed. 'It belongs to a friend of mine and she said you're welcome to use it.'

'That's excellent, Ruby. Is it in the village?'

'No, it's a little way out, I'm afraid. I hope you like peace and quiet. It's an old crofter's cottage that my friend and her husband have been renovating. They're not letting it yet, but they have had some visitors staying there recently. Everything works – the plumbing is all in. All it needs is a bit of painting and some frills. She said you can have it for the same price as we charge. Stay a few days if you want. What do you think?'

It was getting late and Katy was tired. She wanted to load up with food from the village store and get settled in for the night. It sounded fine. Beggars can't be choosers.

'It sounds great. Thank you, Ruby. I really appreciate it. Where exactly is it?'

'Not too far, only a few miles along the road. I'll get Judd to run you up there. It's a short distance from the Commando Monument. You'll get a lovely view of the mountains from there.'

Katy didn't know whether to laugh or cry. It was a real glass half-full, glass half-empty moment. The crofter's cottage was less than two miles away from the site of the lodge where they'd stayed as teenagers.

As Judd drove her up there, talking nonsense all the time, she drifted away into her own thoughts. She had a place to stay and she could remain there until she needed to travel up to Inverness. She'd forget the Great Glen Way now. That idea was abandoned. Finding dead bodies tends to screw up travel plans. She'd catch a bus to Inverness at the end of the week.

She was congratulating herself on her excellent organisation. She'd emailed Emma the details of the cottage and her temporary phone number before she left the B&B. She'd even mentioned the proximity to the lodge, she thought Emma would like that detail. There was little chance that she'd have a decent phone signal up there, let alone broadband access, so she'd thought it best to let her friend know what was going on while she could. Ruby and Judd had an old Windows XP computer in the hallway for guest use, so she logged into her emails and sent her message old style.

They turned off by the monument, passed the start of the track to the lodge and continued a further couple of miles up the road towards the cottage. Katy did her best to clock features along the route so that she could remember where she'd been. It was straightforward. There was only one road, no turn-offs to make, no chance of confusion.

Suddenly Judd stopped and applied the handbrake.

'This is it,' he said. 'The key should be under the doormat.'

Katy had to stop herself laughing. After living in London for years, she couldn't believe that a doormat was still the best home security device available. Ruby hadn't needed to phone her friend, Katy could have just walked in and become a squatter.

Judd helped her carry in her bag and the box that they'd filled with food at the local store. She'd gambled on there being a microwave in the kitchen. She was right. There was no cooker, but a kettle and a microwave. She could survive the apocalypse with those two items – and perhaps her laptop and a decent Wi-Fi signal.

She walked around the cottage. There wasn't much to explore. It was single level with a living–dining area, one bedroom, a small kitchen and a shower room with a toilet. A crofting family probably brought up a family of ten kids in there in years gone by, but Katy thought it was the perfect size for one. Things were looking up. This was good. It was private, quiet and cosy. She had food and a phone. And the view was stunning. Alone at last. No Louis, no Olly, and no obligations. It would be perfect for a day or two. The only drawback was the long walk to the village.

'Have you got everything you need?' Judd asked. He was no doubt anxious to get back to his pal in the bar of the B&B. He'd found the mains switch and the house had fired into life, with most of the lights coming on at once.

'All good,' said Katy. 'Thanks for your help, Judd. And thank Ruby for me too, this place is great.'

Judd left her and she took a second look around. The owners had told her to help herself to bedding and she found a pile of sheets and pillow cases neatly folded in one of the drawers. There was no TV, but they'd been thoughtful enough to leave some books on the shelves. She'd read some trashy novel. That would pass the time. There was even a small patio at the back with a table and chairs, and there was a stunning view of the hills.

After making the bed, microwaving a chicken curry and

finding a book to read, Katy decided to open the patio door at the back of the lounge and eat outside. It was unlocked already. It probably didn't matter in such a rural spot, but she placed her plate and book on the outside table and played with the locking mechanism. She couldn't get it to work. That wasn't good. She didn't want to spend a night alone with a door unlocked.

There was a piece of wood tucked behind the curtain – it fell out while she was moving the door back and forth hoping for some miracle to fix the problem. She realised what it was for straightaway. By closing the door and inserting the wood between one end of the doorframe and the wall, she could secure it fast. Relieved that she'd found a solution, Katy sat outside and ate her meal.

She'd left the Nokia on charge in the kitchen. At first she'd thought the noise she could hear was a bird in the woods, but it was so persistent that at last she realised that someone was calling her. It was Emma.

'Can't I leave you for five minutes without getting into trouble? What happened? I got your email. I read the story online. Was that you, the person who found the body?'

'It's a crap signal, Ems. I've got one bar. If I disappear, it's because I moved five centimetres to the right.'

Katy brought Emma up-to-date. If they'd been sitting in a bar on a Friday night with a bottle of Prosecco in front of them, it would have been like any other night on the town.

'You've got another one of those weird letters,' Emma said when they'd exhausted the topic of the body in the car. 'Do you want me to open it?'

Katy was feeling braver sitting in the solitude of the cottage garden. Whoever it was, they couldn't touch her out there. In London, perhaps, but nobody knew where she was now. She was safe.

'Go on, but be gentle with me. Is it from Leytonstone again? Who the fuck do we know in Leytonstone? Nobody.'

'Sorry, it's more of the same,' Emma said, as if she was responsible for the letter. 'Yes, it is Leytonstone again. All it says is: *Neither of us is without blame.* What's this all about, Katy? It sounds serious to me.'

Katy felt suddenly vulnerable.

'I don't know, Ems. Could it be Louis? He's the only person mad enough to send something like that. But who does he mean when he says "neither of us"?'

'I'm so bloody pleased it was you who copped off with him that night and not me. I wish he'd just fuck off. Bloody hell, the man is a nutter. Do you want me to show these to the police?'

'I wish I had my phone. You could email them to me and I could show DS Buchanan. He'd tell me what to do.'

'I can MMS them to you. What about that?'

'MMS? Isn't that what the cavemen used to do?' Katy laughed.

'I'll give it a try when I've rung off. They'll look small on an old Nokia, but at least you'll be able to show him. The rest of your letters are notifications – gas, electricity, water. Oh, and there's one about the TV licence. They want to know who's living in your old house. I'll post it back through the letterbox and the new owner can pick it up ... Are you still there? Katy?'

'Shh, hang on a sec.'

'Are you okay? Is everything alright?'

'Yes, it's fine, but I thought I heard something. It's getting dark here now. The house is surrounded by wood-land – it must have been a critter. Do they have foxes in Scotland?'

'Don't ask me, I'm only a teacher,' Emma laughed.

'What the fuck do I know? Anyhow, what are your plans now? I assume we're still on for Inverness? I can't wait to spend nine hours on a train. I've been chatting to Sarah. Nathan's away on business, but he'll be back in time. He promised her he'd be there. Izzy said she's still okay too. I think she's forgiven me at last, she sounded quite relaxed about things ... Katy? Katy? Are you there?'

Katy had put the phone down. She was convinced that something – or somebody – was watching her from the woods.

CHAPTER EIGHT

Katy looked out into the half-darkness. There was no fence separating the cottage from the land beyond it. The two ran together as if the garden had been consumed by the surrounding landscape.

She strained her ears. She'd been certain that she was being watched – it had come over her like a panic attack. Part of her wanted to bolt inside the house and barricade herself in, but the braver part of her was angry and ready to confront whoever it was. She cursed Louis. She'd thought she was well shot of him, but this is what crazy men do to a woman. And Olly too. Maybe it was Olly who'd unsettled her more. Katy couldn't shake off the feeling that things weren't quite right with him, but she couldn't put her finger on it.

'Katy? Are you there?'

Emma's voice came through the phone. Katy had left it on the table, completely forgetting her conversation. As she picked it up, a wildcat emerged from the trees. Katy watched it as it ran about a hundred yards ahead of her. It looked like a tabby cat, but she could see that it wasn't. It had a different look about it. The tail was thick, with distinctive black rings around it. That was no domestic animal.

'Hi Emma, yes, I'm fine. I'm a silly cow, that's all. If you ever see Louis again, kick him in the bollocks and tell him, that's from Katy. These fucking men I meet, they're screwing with my mind.'

Katy watched the cat disappear into a patch of gorse.

'So we're all set for Sunday,' she continued. 'Thanks for pulling that together.'

'You should go on my Facebook profile and connect with everybody, if they haven't already sent you friend requests.'

It was getting close to the reunion. Katy felt nervous, but she didn't know why. She'd seen a couple of friend requests waiting before her laptop had been handed over to the police, but something had stopped her from accepting them. It was the thought of them all together in one place ... in *that* place. After that summer they'd stayed in touch, but things had never really been the same again. There was no hostility, they'd just drifted into other friendship groups.

It was Sarah and Nathan who started the change. When they became an item, they pulled out of the planned house share at the last minute. Elijah's room had been re-let already, and some hippy guy called Troy was moving in. Emma and Katy stayed friends, but Izzy, as ever, was very private and moved out well before the end of the first term. She got a flat on her own. She couldn't stand the mess in the shared house. There was no big break up, it simply fell apart.

Katy wondered why they'd arranged the reunion. Partly it was an age thing – past events never seem so bad when viewed in the rear-view mirror. And she needed to know. That summer had screwed them over in so many ways and it was still affecting her life. They were stuck in the events of the past. Nathan and Sarah must have felt it – they were still together. Izzy was still working in the village shop. Emma and Katy ... she paused for a moment. When she was being harsh with herself, she knew that they were like a broken record, stuck in the same old groove and never playing a new song. She'd never seen it with quite so much clarity before. She loved Emma, but Emma was part of the problem, a yoke from the past. She was going to have to let her go.

This get-together was the end. It was a last supper. Something in her subconscious had known it all along, and only now had her conscious mind caught up. This was her divorce from Emma and everybody else in that group. She was shaking the dirt off her boots. This was the ending they should have got all those years back.

She finished the call with Emma, who was completely unaware of her decision. She would see the place where it had all happened one more time to be certain that she remembered it right, but it was over. Emma was part of the problem. She couldn't break away without ditching her best friend. They'd have a great weekend, get pissed and laugh themselves silly. Then she'd disappear abroad, blame poor internet connections and expensive roaming charges and disappear from the picture.

Katy decided not to make the friend connections that Emma had suggested. She would wind down her social media. She was crap at Facebook anyway, Emma had told her as much. She'd stop posting and then delete the account.

It was time to move inside. There was a chill in the air. Katy scanned the trees one last time before closing the patio door behind her and inserting the piece of wood to secure it properly. She pushed on the handle both ways to reassure herself that it couldn't be opened. She was locked in, safe for the night.

One of the things that had surprised her since arriving in Fort William was how used to the London noise she'd become: the roar of traffic, screeching sirens, even the bustle of people. In Scotland all was quiet. The night was still. The only sound that she could hear was the electronic hum of the fridge in the kitchen. It was blissful yet also exposing. She was on her own with no fool of a man to mess things up. The Spice Girls would have her think that it was empowering. A bit of girl power. As she sat on the sofa thinking things through, it felt damn scary.

She was pining for Wi-Fi. There was no way her phone would be receiving data, it could barely hang onto a phone signal out there. Besides, Buchanan's phone was a heap of shit. Fancy making a mobile phone that could only be used to send and receive calls. She scouted around for a router. If they were going to be renting the place out, there had to be one there somewhere. Even anti-city types needed their Wi-Fi, if only to catch up on the latest from Pornhub. Eventually she found one in the kitchen drawer, along with a box of unopened kitchen knives and a corkscrew. It hadn't been unpacked yet and the phone line still wasn't connected. It was just a white wire stuck through a window frame. She'd have to settle for the book that she'd picked out earlier. She was going back to the Dark Ages.

As it turned out, Katy didn't get much reading done that night. She began to read on the sofa, but didn't last more than five pages before she was out like a light.

It was the bump of the book dropping onto the floor that startled her from her sleep. She was hot and sweaty, her mouth gummed up with whatever gunk it is that comes out to play in the night. She'd been asleep for some time. It was completely dark. You never got darkness like that in London.

There was a noise, a persistent low mechanical noise. She tried to home in on the sound, but she was still struggling to wake up. Then she saw it: the piece of wood that she'd jammed in the door had dropped out onto the floor. A rush of adrenalin shook her out of her daze. And that sound that she could hear? It was the low growl of a car engine running outside the cottage. She was no longer alone.

The cottage was in complete darkness except for the glow of sidelights reflected in the windows. The car was waiting, ready to drive off at any moment. Was it the police, maybe hoping to catch her awake still? Not at past two o' clock in the morning it wasn't. Could it be a lost tourist searching for a campsite late at night? Maybe they were studying a map, perhaps considering knocking on the door and asking for directions.

Katy wondered whether she should phone Buchanan, but decided to watch and wait. There had been no movement, no slamming of car doors, only the rumble of the engine on the road outside. She couldn't make out the colour or even the type of car. Then, without warning, it suddenly drove off.

She started to breathe again. She hadn't realised how tense she'd been. Katy would never have described herself as nervous or paranoid, but perhaps her time with Louis had had more effect on her than she'd thought. It had only been a car pulled up outside after all. She despised herself that her first thought had been to find a cupboard or closet to hide in. Memories of Louis's angry attempts to break into her house had come flooding back.

She thought about the piece of wood jammed in the patio door. Is that what had woken her up? She'd heard the book thump on the floor, but the wood must have dropped out of the frame first, shaking her out of her sleep. She went over to investigate – it would need to be wedged in at more of an angle. It was a really cack-handed way of keeping that back door secure.

She would need to speak to Buchanan, share her worries with him and get some reassurance. She told herself she was being foolish, but she was rattled.

The next day Katy got up late and was eating Coco Pops at eleven o' clock, tired and irritable after her disturbed night. She'd forced herself to stay in bed, dropping off again at seven o'clock or thereabouts, and then sleeping until the morning was almost gone. The birdsong was ridiculously loud and disturbed her more than the London traffic used to. She couldn't believe that she'd polished off three bowls of cereal. She was famished. She'd get an arse on her if she kept eating like that. Maybe more hiking wasn't such a bad idea if she was going to start finding solace in sugary breakfasts now she was living a nomadic lifestyle.

She showered and rinsed out some knickers and a T-shirt in the sink. There was no washing powder, so she used washing-up liquid instead. There was a small washing line outside, and she hung her few clothes out to dry before heading off to walk the short distance to the track leading to the site of the lodge.

As Katy followed the narrow road, she thought over the

next few days. Things weren't going to plan. It was silly to keep walking backwards and forwards, and it made even less sense to stay in Spean Bridge. She should have headed back to Fort William, checked back in with Paige – if her room was free – and hired a car. Not for the first time since she left London, she cursed her lack of forethought. Roger Parry's death had changed everything. The decisions she had taken had seemed sensible at the time, but as she walked along the road with only nature's chorus to accompany her, it was clear that she needed to do things differently.

Katy arrived at the point where the track left the road. It had only been a thirty-minute walk from the cottage, not too bad. From what she could remember, not much had changed. There used to be a five-bar wooden gate, but the posts had been replaced and it was now a sturdier and more functional metal structure. She remembered that because Izzy had been able to squeeze her moped through a gap at the sides, whereas the rest of them had had to open and close the gate to get the car through. In the end, they'd given up and left it open. Now it was completely enclosed, there would be no squeezing through at the sides.

There was a Private Property sign on the gate. That hadn't been there before. It wasn't locked though – there was no need to lock anything out there. Even so, she decided to climb over it, and laughed to herself as she messed up her footing and landed awkwardly on the other side. It wasn't quite Total Wipeout winning contestant stuff – she would open the gate next time.

The track was as long as she remembered it and lined with trees. She wondered what possessed people to live in places like that. London ground to a halt with an inch of snow, but what would it be like out here when the weather got bad? No wonder it had taken the fire brigade so long to get there. What had made them holiday in that place? Only student naivety could explain it – and the fact that Google Maps hadn't been invented. In the nineties it would have been almost impossible to see quite how remote it was before they went.

Finally, the track ended and she came into the clearing where the lodge had been. It was a stunning outlook, quite breathtaking in fact. Her younger self hadn't appreciated that. She'd been too busy looking for opportunities to sneak off for a quickie with Elijah. Scenery wasn't the first thing on her mind back then.

Katy surveyed the area, trying to remember how it had been set out. She had her backpack with her, and the photos were still inside. She pulled them out and tried to position herself roughly where the photographer had been standing. They were poor quality compared to the ones you'd be able to take on a smart phone.

The lodge had been levelled, and there was nothing left of the original building. A one-storey brick structure had been put in its place, but it was unfinished. There were no windows or roof, only bricks and concrete blocks, the skeleton of a wooden roof frame and a lot of debris left around the place. It wasn't even a work in progress, it had all been abandoned some time ago. Whoever owned it must simply have lacked the will to finish the project. They'd given up and left it. Maybe their money had run out, who knew?

Did Elijah's ghost still walk this place? Katy wasn't superstitious, but the thought of there being some afterlife or spiritual presence fascinated her. If he could talk to her now, would he blame her? Could she have done more to make things right that day?

Katy replaced the photos in her bag, holding one back for reference. She walked up to the abandoned construction to see if it was safe to walk inside. There weren't any builder's signs, no nods to health and safety, it was completely open. Besides, who would even know it was there from the road?

Katy walked through what should have been the front entrance. It had a wooden frame loosely attached to the brickwork, but no door. The concrete floor was covered with lichen. Nature was trying its best to claim the building as its own. It would have made a nice holiday lodge once completed. It was quite a size, as their wooden structure had been: a bungalow with three bedrooms as far as she could tell. There was even a bath in one of the rooms, still packed in cardboard and plastic, and resting upright against the wall.

She wandered into what would have been the kitchen. The units had been delivered and left there, still wrapped up in polythene. Katy tried to date them from their design. They weren't modern, that was for sure. Then an unexpected sight. Somebody had been using the stacked units as a table. Resting on top was a half-smoked cigarette, a can of coke, not fully drunk, and a packet of crisps. These must have been left recently, very recently in fact. Coke would evaporate, surely? How long for crisps to rot? These looked fresh to her. A closer look at the packet showed that the sell-by date was still current.

Suddenly Katy felt vulnerable. She had that same uncertainty she'd experienced when she thought she was being watched at the crofter's cottage. She reached into her pocket for the Nokia. Could she get a signal out there? No, of course not.

She looked around. She was alone, she was sure of that.

There was no sign of any vehicle, but somebody had been there. A tramp perhaps? But who would even know the bungalow existed? This was Louis again, screwing with her head. It was probably the owner. Why couldn't it be a simple explanation like that? Louis was making her paranoid.

She'd have to be careful. Buchanan would think she was some crazy lady if she started reading things into everyday situations. Take Olly, for instance. He was a nice guy, but within twenty-four hours of shagging him, she was convinced he was a stalker. She'd have to watch herself. This is how bastards like Louis kept their power.

There was a mechanical sound in the distance. At first she thought it was a chainsaw, but it persisted and it was getting closer. Katy stepped outside the half-built house to see if she could figure out where it was coming from. This might be her explanation for the coke can and crisps.

It was a motorcycle. Quite a powerful one at that, but not running at speed. It was coming up the track, the revs were low, but it was definitely a motorcycle. Katy didn't know what to do. She was an adult, for God's sake. There was no need to hide. She had a perfectly good reason for being there and if it was the owner they'd understand.

As the powerful black bike emerged at the end of the track, she decided to conceal herself anyway. The rider was tall and rode with confidence, covered from top to toe in black leathers. Katy ducked behind a stack of bricks at the side of the house and watched as he stopped the engine and climbed off the bike.

The rider seemed as interested in the site as Katy was. It

was difficult to get a clear look at his face. It seemed he hadn't decided whether to stay: he'd kept his helmet on, just lifting the visor. He took in the scene while Katy remained hidden behind the bricks – she'd have to stay out of sight. She'd look ridiculous if she stepped out now.

Then he took his helmet off, but since he was wearing a black fabric helmet liner underneath, it was still impossible to have a good look at his face. He walked around where only minutes earlier Katy had been examining her photo. Then, as if resolving to stay a while, he removed the helmet liner, strolled back over to the bike and placed it inside the helmet.

'Turn around, you bugger. Let's get a good look at you,' Katy whispered under her breath. The rider was teasing her. He walked to the side of the half-built structure, up to the door, and then around the other side, close to where Katy was hiding. She came up with her excuse. If she was caught, she'd say she'd been exploring the woodland area that surrounded the clearing and got lost. He was only a couple of metres away from her now. If he would only turn around, she could finally see him close-up.

When he did, Katy let out a shriek. She knocked a brick from the stack she was hiding behind and he jumped back, startled. Only it wasn't a he. It was a she. And it was somebody that Katy knew, somebody she knew very well.

'Izzy? Is that you?'

'You frightened the life out of me! I can't believe it – Katy Wild! You've barely changed. What are you doing here?'

Of course, Isobel knew the answer to that question. It would be the same reason she was there. She was paying a visit to the ghosts of the past.

Isobel and Katy hadn't seen each other since graduation

day in 2001. They'd kept loosely in touch, exchanging Christmas cards every year, but it was Emma who was the sociable one, making connections on Facebook, sustaining the flimsy communications over the years. There was a moment of awkwardness before they moved towards each other for a hug.

'What brought you down here?' Katy asked. 'Have you been back since?'

'I've been to the end of the track a couple of times, but not up to where the lodge was. I could never bring myself to do it. I came here today to prepare myself for Inverness at the weekend. It seemed like the right time to do it.'

'I can't believe we met like this,' Katy replied, 'though I guess it's not that weird. It's pretty well the first place any of us would head if we were back in the area. Are you still living in the same village? What is it, half an hour from here?'

'Even less on the bike,' Izzy smiled. 'Remember that old moped I used to ride? This thing goes about four times the speed. It's my day off today and I thought I'd head over here. I wanted to see it again before we all met up. Actually, if I'm honest, I wanted to see it before I met you.'

Katy looked at Isobel. As a student, she'd been tense and uptight. To be fair, they probably all were at that age. She'd relaxed and her face had lost the hostility of her younger years. She appeared to be a lot more comfortable in her own skin now. What she said was fair enough. Katy had lost her boyfriend, and it had been a horrible time for all of them. They would all have a lot of thinking to do before they met up again.

'You look good, Izzy,' Katy said, and she meant it. 'How are things with you?'

'Did you know I got married last year?'

'No, I didn't know. That's something Emma didn't tell me.'

'She probably didn't know. I made the photos restricted on Facebook. It wasn't a big deal.'

'Who's the lucky guy?' The minute the words left her mouth, Katy knew she'd fucked up.

'Lady. The lucky lady. You must know I'm gay. Hadn't you figured it out back then?'

Katy backpedalled and made an even bigger mess of it.

'I didn't know. I do now though. I mean, I just figured it out. Not this minute ... Jesus, Katy, shut your mouth. Look, Isobel, I didn't know back then, I do now and I'm so happy for you. I really am.'

She meant it too. It was no wonder Izzy had been so uptight if she'd felt she had to hide something as big as that from them.

'Actually, I'm not sure I even knew when we were at uni,' Isobel said, deciding to put Katy out of her misery. 'It's funny. It was when we came here that I really began to doubt myself. Emma must have told you what happened.'

Katy nodded.

'They were different times back then,' she continued, the severity that Katy remembered returning to her face. 'Mum was still alive, and she'd never have forgiven me. She wouldn't have understood. Later I had to keep my relationship with Nancy under wraps for five years right under Mum's nose – she was the one who'd employed her to work in the shop. We run it together now, and we're married, and nobody gives a shit anymore. But I wish I could have told Mum before she died.'

Katy squeezed her arm. She wondered whether Izzy's mum had known all along.

'Are you staying for a while?' Isobel asked. 'Now we're here, we may as well have a catch-up.'

'I'd love to,' Katy said, relieved to find a friend. She hadn't been sure how things would be with Isobel, but it felt good to see her again. What had she been so afraid of?

'How about we go to that Little Chef we used to go to? It's reopened as a café.'

'That would be perfect. Shall I meet you there? I'll have to walk. I haven't got any transport.'

'Sod that!' Izzy laughed. 'You're coming on the back of the bike, if you're willing to take a chance of being caught without a helmet on. I won't go fast. Moped speed, I promise.'

Katy laughed too. This was nothing like the Isobel that she remembered. She was chilled out, relaxed. She was even a law-breaker. Katy wasn't sure if she was up for a ride without a helmet – it seemed to be a bit on the wild side, but she'd take a chance. It wasn't as if the cops were on every corner, and it was only a few miles.

'You want to take a look around first? I was in the middle of it when you arrived. I thought you might be the owner. I'm ashamed to say that I was hiding from you.'

'It's good to see that you haven't completely grown up, Katy. I always wanted to have more fun back then. I had a broomstick stuck up my arse in those days.'

They walked through the house. It was a fairly pointless exercise. There was nothing left of the previous structure, and the layout was completely different. It was only when they came to the back door that they spotted something that was familiar to them both.

'Bloody hell! Look, that old patio is still there.'

Isobel was pointing, but Katy had less reason to recall it than Izzy.

'When I think of the time I spent out here smoking like a chimney. I've stopped now. I met Nancy, she didn't like the smell and I stopped dead. Just like that. This brings back memories. You know this is where I was before the fire broke out?'

She said this tentatively, as if she wasn't sure how Katy would react to talk of the fire. She seemed keen to raise it, even though it was such a touchy subject.

'No, I can't remember who was where,' Katy replied. 'It doesn't really matter now though, does it?'

'It does to me,' Isobel said, suddenly very serious. 'This is where I started the fire. With a bloody cigarette!'

CHAPTER NINE

Katy climbed onto the back of the motorbike. She was still stunned by what Izzy had told her. It was such a simple fact, yet it had so much impact on what had happened.

Isobel handled the machine with confidence and expertise. It felt huge to Katy, who was concerned that it would fall over.

'Put your hands around my waist and move with me when I lean. Oh, and close your mouth or you'll end up with it full of bugs.'

She smiled at that one and started up the engine. Katy watched how she did it. She hadn't got a clue how motorbikes worked, she'd never been on one and they were alien to her.

'Ready?' Isobel asked. 'I promise I won't go fast, and you make sure to let me know if you're scared or want me to slow down. Okay? Here we go.'

Katy watched as Izzy flicked through the gears with her foot and then pulled back the throttle. She rode steadily and slowly and it wasn't too long before Katy was enjoying the experience. With such an expert handler in control of the ride, it was fine, nothing to worry about.

They made it to what they'd known as the Little Chef without being spotted by the police. There was little chance of that in such a rural area, but as law-abiding citizens Isobel and Katy knew they were taking a calculated risk.

The café wasn't quite as Katy remembered. She'd been certain it fronted onto the river – that's how she recalled its location. The river was nearby, but not so close that you could look out over it. Funny how memories get jumbled, she thought. She could have sworn that's what it looked like.

Although the building was no longer branded as a Little Chef, it was clear that's what it had once been. Now it was a café, with a change of colour palette, some modern furniture and the kind of menu that makes you wonder why you don't eat a fry-up for breakfast every morning. Coco Pops had seemed like a good option at the time, but Katy was starving and a bacon and egg roll was exactly what she needed. Besides, what Izzy had told her had made her mind race into overdrive. That was another day she hadn't remembered correctly.

With an order placed and a couple of comfy chairs secured, they continued their conversation. Katy had been glad of the time on the bike. It had given her an opportunity to think it all through.

'Recovered from the ride?' Izzy smiled.

She was so much more at ease than when they'd been younger. Nancy was obviously good for her.

'You've certainly graduated from that moped of yours. Why do you still ride bikes rather than use a car?'

'Nancy has a car, and we use it when we're out together, but it's not only middle-aged guys with beer guts who like the thrill of the open road. I've always loved it. It makes me feel alive. Driving a car is dreary in comparison.'

Katy didn't want to talk about bikes. She wanted to discuss the fire.

'So, was that cigarette the official reason for the fire starting?' she asked, pulling a handbrake turn on the topic of conversation.

'Didn't you read the report? Yes, and I've lived with it every day since.'

'But it was an accident. I can't believe how much wood there was in that cabin. That must have been a fire hazard, a disaster waiting to happen.'

Isobel shrugged.

'I know there were a lot of other factors involved in Elijah's death, but I was patient zero. I thought you knew that?'

'I never read the report – I was too upset. My dad did a Reader's Digest job on it and told me the main details, so I knew they thought it was a cigarette that had started the fire. But I seem to recall that they weren't completely sure, and I did think it was unusual that it was in the room Elijah was in. He never smoked, he hated it.'

'I was outside the window, remember? I was on the patio of doom sulking about something or other and Elijah and Nathan were chatting in the bedroom. Everything suddenly went a bit tense in there, and the next thing they were fighting. I stubbed my cigarette out on the bench and flicked it away, but it must have gone through the bedroom window. I didn't realise what I'd done, of course. They pieced it together after the fire.'

'God, Izzy. That's a terrible thing to live with. It's a good thing I didn't hear this back then – I'm not sure I'd have been so understanding when I was younger. But that can't be the whole story. The cigarette might have started the fire, but the rest of us got out. Elijah died because he got stuck in that bloody room. For some reason, he didn't manage to escape. That was what was always the mystery to me. Why didn't he just walk away like the rest of us?'

'And I never really understood how that cigarette could have started any fire. You know what we were like back then: poor students who smoked their cigarettes until there was no tobacco left. I was certain it was out, but they reckoned that it must have smouldered and fired back up again.'

They sat in silence for a few minutes, mulling it over. The tea and butties arrived. They were a useful distraction.

'I know about you and Emma, by the way. That's something else I only just found out. I don't care, and I wouldn't have cared then. Emma can be a bit flighty at times – it gets her into trouble with men too. She lines them up and then lets them down. Sounds like that's what she did to you.'

Izzy nodded slowly, as if the memory was a painful one.

'I wasn't entirely sure I was gay. Don't forget this was before the internet. You couldn't read it up on Google and check out other people's experiences. It involved a lot more introspection and self-loathing back then. Emma was a cow. I still think she was a cow. It was a bit of fun to her, a summer fling, but it was more than that to me. When she ended it like that, I was hurt and angry. I still think she behaved really badly.'

'I agree,' Katy replied. 'She doesn't mean it, but she doesn't think. That was horrible what she did to you. We were all shitty back then. I guess we were all young and stupid.'

'Agreed. Now we're old and stupid!'

'Well, you did alright. You've got Nancy. Look at me and Ems. Still getting sloshed on Prosecco on a Friday night and not a husband in sight. These eggs won't last forever, you know. They'll be past their sell-by date soon.'

'Emma told me about your bloke when we connected on Facebook. Nobody deserves a wanker like that. He didn't hit you, did he?'

'No. Only once. It was psychological. I let it run on too long, and I should have ended it way before I did. But you know the drill – I was scared and hoped he'd stop it. I was stupid. Anyway, it's over now, although I'm not sure Louis has got the message.'

'He's still bothering you? The little shit!'

Izzy looked really angry at that. Katy calmed her down.

'No, no, he's out of my life now. Why do you think I'm hiding up here? He won't bother me again. He doesn't know where I am.'

She decided to change the subject. A dollop of egg ran along the side of her roll and narrowly missed her legs. She wiped it with a paper napkin.

'How are Sarah and Nathan? Do you see them?'

'Why does everybody assume that we all know each other in Scotland? They're miles away. Aberdeen is still a hefty drive from here. It's a hefty drive from anywhere! It's almost two hundred miles from my place. But no. To answer your question, I don't see them. You know there wasn't much love lost between me and Sarah. She was so militant at college. And I'll never know why she and Nathan ended up together. You must know he's gay.'

Katy almost spat out the bacon that she was chewing.

'So what the hell is he doing with Sarah?'

'I didn't know why Sarah was always chasing him. I got the surprise of my life when they got together after the fire. Nathan fancied Elijah. Couldn't you see that? He was in love with Elijah.'

Katy had to stop eating. She put down her roll and thought it through.

'There's no way he was in love with Elijah. I mean, everybody loved him, he was that kind of guy. But romantic love? Come on!'

She doubted her own words, even as they were coming out of her mouth. What had Buchanan told her? But it seemed impossible. That's not how she remembered it.

'They always were an odd couple. Sarah seemed to want to bag him for herself, and that appeared to be her only objective. Nowadays Nathan works in IT and is away from home most of the time. I know they don't have any children. Odd that, isn't it? Nancy and I want kids. It's the most natural thing on earth when you're in love.'

'All sorts of shit can stop people having kids. It's not obligatory, you know.'

Katy had felt the kid pressure herself, so she was a bit forceful with her response. She decided to cool things down a bit.

'Do you want to come back to the cottage for a catch-up? It's great to see you and it seems a shame to go our separate ways so soon. To be honest, I was nervous about seeing everybody again, but this is good, I'm enjoying this.'

'I'd love to,' Izzy said. 'I'll need to ring home to let everybody know. Karen can stay on to cash up the till, I'm sure she'll be okay with that. Yes, let's do it. It'll be fun.'

As Izzy opened the contacts book on her phone, Katy looked up towards the door. She'd been aware of people coming in and out of the café, but somebody had caught her attention while they'd been talking. It was Buchanan and he was heading over to their table. He looked like he was about to deliver bad news.

Isobel sensed that something was up and cut short her call.

'I know you from somewhere,' she said as Buchanan pulled up a chair.

'DS Buchanan was one of the officers who attended the fire,' Katy replied. 'There's something I haven't even had time to tell you yet, Izzy. I expect that's what this is about.'

'Hi, yes. Ruby said I'd find you here. She said she spotted you riding a massive black motorcycle through the village without a helmet. Is that right?'

Katy looked sheepish.

'I'm only teasing, but don't get caught and for God's sake don't fall off. I've seen what happens to riders when they're wearing a helmet, so believe me, you wouldn't want to come off a bike without one.'

Katy nodded. She liked Buchanan. He was speaking to her out of genuine concern for her wellbeing.

'I take it you're not here to give us a road safety lesson?'

'I'm afraid not. Are you okay for me to talk in front of your friend?'

'I'm Isobel. I think I can just about remember you from the fire.'

Buchanan shook her hand.

'Go on,' said Katy. 'Izzy will be as interested in this as I am.'

'I'm sorry to have to tell you that Roger Parry's death has now turned into a murder investigation.'

'Damn it, Katy. What haven't you been telling me?'

'It's a long story, Izzy. Roger Parry was Elijah's old tutor. We were supposed to meet at the monument and I found him dead in his car.'

'My God! I'm beginning to think this place is cursed.'

'You and me both,' Katy replied. 'So what happened?'

'He was strangled from behind with his own belt. We think it was opportunistic rather than planned. The car is a rental, so that makes the DNA situation difficult and there were no witnesses – it's too busy a spot for anybody to be taking any notice, and with the tinted glass they wouldn't have seen anything even if they had been looking. We're at a bit of a dead end.'

'So you think it was random, some nutter on the loose?'

'We don't think Parry was masturbating in the car. We suspect that was set up as a distraction. Neither do we think it was a sex game gone wrong. It doesn't feel right. He made two calls to the same number in the hour before it happened. It seems likely that he'd arranged to meet somebody else at the monument, as well as you. Your calls are all logged as you outlined in your statement.'

'Why don't you think it was a sex thing? It sounds like some sort of Tinder liaison gone wrong to me.'

Katy was trying to sound calm, but inside she was scared. She was thinking about the wildcat the previous night, and then there was the food and cigarette at the site of the lodge.

'Parry placed calls to a virtual number. It was one of these disposable numbers that you can rent online. We can't trace the owner, they covered their tracks. This is either somebody who takes not being outed very seriously or someone who has something to hide. It might have been about sex, but copper's intuition says not.'

'I don't know what to say.' Katy was taken aback. She didn't know where this left her.

Isobel seemed equally shocked.

'I certainly picked a good day to visit. You're not very good for the local tourism industry, Katy.'

She realised she'd been too flippant too soon and reached out to touch Katy's arm.

'Sorry. That was a stupid thing to say. You okay?'

'Yes, I'm fine. Are you suggesting that some loony is on the loose? If so I'm not sure about being in that cottage by myself.'

'You certainly need to take care. Since you were also there to meet Parry in that car park, there's a chance that the two things might be connected.'

'That's good to know.'

She couldn't stop thinking about the patio door and the piece of wood. She considered telling Buchanan what had happened, but she didn't want to appear to be over-reacting. After all, what *had* happened? A piece of wood had slipped out of a window frame and a car had pulled up while the driver looked at a map for directions. She was being silly.

'I'm happy to come back to the house with you,' Isobel offered. 'I'll stay overnight if it helps, or you can stay with us at Glenfinnan. That might be a better solution.'

Katy checked the clock on the wall. It was late already. She'd intended to get that patio door looked at or move back to Paige's place in Fort William. And hire a car. Meeting Isobel had messed up her plans for the day.

'That might not be such a bad idea, Izzy. Could you head up to the cottage and start to get my stuff together? I'll go with DS Buchanan to Judd and Ruby's to see if they have a room for tonight. If the B&B's full, I'll come back home with you.'

She looked at Buchanan.

'I'm guessing you'd prefer me to stay local rather than go walkabout?'

'Yes, it would be useful if you could stay around for another day or two so I can find you if I need to. I'll run you back to the cottage to meet your friend here once we're done at the B&B. And you'll need a motorcycle helmet if you go on the bike. You can't ride all the way up to Glenfinnan without one.'

'The key is under the doormat, Izzy. Please don't start telling me about security – I know! It's a couple of miles down the road from where our holiday lodge was. You can't miss it, it's on the corner and tucked in from the road. I'll phone you when we're on our way.'

The arrangements were set. They paid the bill and left, Izzy roaring off on her bike and Buchanan walking with Katy to his car.

They got in and he sat with his hand ready to turn the key.

'I'm glad I've got you on your own. I wanted a word in private, without having to go through the hassle of making it formal at the station.'

'Go on. What is it?'

'You know what I said about that virtual phone number earlier?'

'Yes. How does that work? How can someone use a phone number that isn't registered?'

'It's simple enough. It works like disposable mobile phones. So long as you buy them with cash and don't get caught on CCTV, there's no way of tying it to you. If we can place the phone with a particular person we can use call records and phone masts, but if we can't link the two, we're shafted. It's the same with virtual phone numbers. You have to use an account, but if you use false details and one of those credit cards with pre-loaded credit, you can manage it.'

'So what was it you wanted to ask me?'

The procedural stuff was all very interesting, but it

wasn't what he'd come to speak to her about, and she needed to get her accommodation sorted out. She didn't want to be in that cottage again after nightfall.

'The virtual phone account was registered to an unusual address. We still can't trace it. Mind you, there are over one hundred businesses registered at the same one. But it didn't quite ring true, not seeing as we're all the way up here in Scotland.'

'So where was it? Anywhere interesting?'

'They're using a virtual office space in east London. Does Leytonstone mean anything to you?'

***

Katy put all notions of being a hysterical female aside and told Buchanan everything. She'd been certain it was Louis sending those letters. It wasn't out of the question that he could post letters from Leytonstone, it was only a short diversion along the Central Line.

'This is really important. It means that everything points to Parry's murder being connected with you, Katy. Have you any idea what might have prompted it?'

They were still sitting in the stationary car, and Buchanan still had his hand on the key.

'I honestly thought it was my fuckwit of an ex – I couldn't see who else it could be. But now I'm not sure. Perhaps it's connected with me returning to Scotland. I'm raking over old coals and maybe somebody wants the past left in the past.'

'It seems clear that somebody didn't want you to talk to Roger Parry. Where are the letters now? Do you have them back at the cottage?'

'I have one of them in my bag. I put it in there the other

day. Give me a minute, it's stuffed into one of the side pockets.'

Katy leant over to the back seat of the car where she'd thrown the bag. She fumbled around inside, found the letter and handed it to Buchanan.

'Emma gave me this before I left, and she has another at her house. She texted me a photo of it, but it won't be very good on that old Nokia. Do you want to keep this one?'

'Yes, it's unlikely that we'll find anything useful on it now, but I need to hang on to it. You do know you need to find somewhere less isolated to stay tonight, Katy? You can't stay in the cottage, that's a bad idea now. We have to get you somewhere among people – and I want you to call me if you have any worries at all.'

She nodded. She was beginning to wish that she'd stayed in London. At least Louis limited his activities to trying to bash doors down in the middle of the night. If there was a killer about, she was right out of her depth.

'I'm beginning to think that you should go with your friend Izzy out of the village. It might be best if only you and I know where you're staying.'

'Yes, let's do that,' Katy replied. 'I'd feel safer that way. How will I get there? Can you give me a lift ... unless you don't mind me riding pillion on her motorbike, of course.'

Buchanan smiled.

'I could see if someone from the station could drive you ... but no, I'll do it myself. Let's keep quiet about this for now.

'You've not been posting or tweeting about any of this, have you? People forget how revealing that stuff can be.'

'No, I'm still stuck with your damn phone – and under one pound of credit. I haven't had internet access for a while now and it's killing me. But I don't know if anybody else has said anything on Facebook.'

'Okay, let's join your friend back at the cottage. You can get a phone signal there, right?'

'Yes, it's dodgy, but I can get a signal there. If I wrap myself in tin foil and point south it's actually quite a good one.'

Buchanan smiled again. He didn't remember liking this woman as much when she was younger. She was forgettable then, just a bland, upset teenager.

He turned the key in the ignition and they were on their way. As they drove he gave clear instructions: Katy was to wait at the house with Izzy while he returned to the station with the letter and gave the team an update on the Leytonstone connection. They'd already put more officers out on the roads. They were looking for a killer now, if he – or she – was still around.

'People think it's easy policing this area,' he said, chatty now, 'but it's a pain in the arse with all the tourists. If it's some local bad lad, it's usually simple to sort out, but if it's someone passing through ...Well, that's a devil to get a grip on. There are strange cars in and out of this area all the time.'

Katy was miles away. She was trying to think back to the fire. What was going on? Who would even know she was back in the area, apart from friends on social media?

They arrived at the cottage. Izzy's bike was parked outside.

'Go inside, lock yourselves in and only answer the door to me. You've got my number in your phone so call if you need me. Even if you call without speaking and the credit's used up, I'll come straight back. I'll be one hour max. Can you stay safe until then?'

Katy felt silly even discussing it. How dangerous could it be out there? It was fine. Izzy was with her and she had a phone.

'Thanks for the lift. See you in an hour.' She retrieved her bag from the car.

'Stay put and lock the door. One hour!' Buchanan turned the car around and drove off. Katy waved and then started to make her way towards the front door. The hot metal of Izzy's engine was still clicking as it cooled down from its recent run. The light was beginning to fade. Katy wasn't sure where the day had gone. Buchanan would be back before dark, and she'd soon be safely locked up at Izzy's house.

The front door was slightly ajar when she got there. She was surprised that Isobel hadn't come out to investigate when the car had pulled up.

'Hi Izzy, it's only me!'

Nothing.

She checked the bathroom. Nothing.

'Izzy!'

Katy walked into the lounge area. Isobel had gathered some of her belongings in the centre of the coffee table. Then she saw it in the corner, the piece of wood that had been used to hold the door shut was lying splintered on the floor. Either the patio door had been forced or Isobel had got into a fix trying to get out to retrieve Katy's knickers from the washing line.

Katy walked hesitantly towards the door. It had been pulled shut. Her washing was still on the line, Izzy hadn't made it that far.

'Izzy!'

Katy's calls were becoming more desperate now. Her hand moved down to the phone in her pocket. She hesitated. She wouldn't call Buchanan yet. There was probably a simple explanation.

Katy opened the patio door and stepped out into the garden. No Izzy. Smoke rose from a cigarette lying on the paving slabs, but Izzy had said she'd stopped smoking. She reached for her phone and searched through the contacts to find Buchanan's number.

'Jesus fucking Christ!' she shouted as the call went to voicemail.

Hi, you've reached the voicemail of Detective Superintendent Alan Buchanan. I can't take your call at the moment. Please leave a message and I'll get back to you straightaway.

'It's me, Katy. Get back here! The minute you get this message, get back to the cottage. Izzy's gone. The cottage is empty. Somebody broke in. Come quickly!'

She ended the call. How much credit did she have? Bloody phone, it was worse than useless. Who else could she ring? Emma. She had Emma's number in her message log. She picked up immediately.

'Hi, it's Emma—'

'Emma. It's Katy. Don't talk, just listen. I'm almost out of credit. I'm in trouble. It's a long story. I met Izzy ... she went to the cottage ... she's gone. There's some nutter on the loose. I tried to call the police. Call the police at Fort William. Ask for DS Buchanan—'

The phone went dead.

'Fuck it!' Katy shouted, throwing the phone onto the grass. She stormed back through the house and ran out onto the road. There was no sign of any traffic.

She paused for breath. She had to calm down. Izzy was gone and she'd found a cigarette still smoking at the back of the house. There'd been a cigarette in the half-built bungalow on the site of the lodge. She guessed that the same person was responsible for both and that they must have taken Izzy back there. It must be connected to Elijah and the fire. They'd passed a white car as they'd driven along the road towards the cottage.

Buchanan would pick up the call the minute his phone signal switched back in. He knew where to come. And Emma wasn't stupid, she'd call the police at Fort William. Somebody would be there within ten minutes. Although she hadn't a clue how to ride it, Katy had Izzy's bike and could be up the road in a minute. The keys were on the coffee table, next to her stuff.

She ran inside the house, tore a panel from the Coco Pops packet and scribbled a message on it: *Gone to the lodge. Be careful. Katy*

She grabbed the keys. Picking up a small kitchen knife for protection, she tucked it blade up at the back of her waistband. She rested the makeshift cardboard message by the side of the front door where it wouldn't be missed. She climbed onto the motorcycle. Whoever had taken Izzy, whatever this was about, it was time to put the past behind them. These ghosts had to be laid to rest.

CHAPTER TEN

Katy felt the weight of the motorcycle beneath her. She had to press on, Izzy could be in real trouble. The police would be there soon, and if she was lucky she'd see Buchanan coming down the road. He said he'd drop everything to get back to her.

She thought back to how Isobel had started up the bike. She could barely stand astride it and support it beneath her. Was she being ridiculous to think that she could use it to rescue her friend? She inserted the key and turned it. A light had gone on. Good. She flicked a switch. Izzy had pulled the lever as well – that had to be the clutch. The bike roared into life. The revving was easy, she knew how to do that.

She thought of Izzy and told herself to stop messing around. The gears were going to be the hard bit. And not falling over. Operating the gears herself was completely different to watching Izzy do it. The sheer coordination of it was the biggest challenge. With a leap of faith, Katy moved the gear lever with her foot, revved up, and the bike moved forward. It felt like having a rocket underneath her. She could feel the power in the engine, even though she was crawling along at snail's pace.

Balancing was easier than she thought. She was on the road now. She had to go faster. The engine was being over-revved, and sounded like it was in pain. She attempted another gear change. A squeeze of the clutch, a flick of her foot, and she picked up speed again. The engine immediately sounded more comfortable. Katy attempted the operation twice more. As she moved the throttle, her confidence grew. The bike felt lighter and easier to keep upright when she was moving. She'd figure out how to stop when it came to it.

In a few minutes she was back at the track to the lodge. She decided to head straight up to the bungalow. The gate was already open, Izzy had to be there. She hoped Buchanan would notice that and work out where she'd gone.

As she bumped over the uneven surface she managed to drop a gear and travel at a lower speed. For an instant she felt the exhilaration of riding a powerful machine, but her fear soon returned as she reached the clearing at the top of the track. There was a white SUV parked in front of the partly completed bungalow, its doors wide open. She could see movement in the house.

Katy's foot flicked the gears as she dropped down to first, and then managed to bring the bike to a halt. With the momentum gone, she lost her footing as she tried to take the weight of the machine. The motorcycle began to fall to the ground, and it took all of her strength to support it and pull it up again. Once it was straightened and she had her balance, she felt around for the stand with her foot.

Whoever was with Isobel would know that she was there. If the purr of the engine hadn't alerted them, Katy's undignified arrival certainly would have. She managed to put the bike on its stand and decided to leave it idling. It seemed the prudent thing to do – she and Izzy might need to get away fast, hopefully with Izzy doing the driving.

Katy felt for the kitchen knife and was relieved to find that it hadn't shaken loose during the ride over. She clutched it in her right hand.

'Hello ...' she said tentatively. 'Izzy?'

She walked through the front door frame. There were no voices and no sign of movement.

'Izzy? Jesus Christ! Izzy!'

Standing precariously on an upside-down tea chest, a rope attached to one of the exposed roof joists and looped around her neck, was Isobel. She was silently crying, terrified, unable to let out a sound. Her body was paralysed with fear. If the box tipped or she lost her footing, the noose would pull tight and choke her of life.

Katy rushed towards her. Isobel flinched, fearful that Katy would knock her over.

'That's far enough!'

The voice was familiar, but she couldn't place it.

'Walk away from Izzy. Stand by the window with your back to me.'

'The police will be here soon, you're wasting your time.'

'Shut the fuck up. You always did talk too much.'

He knew Isobel as Izzy, he knew *her*. It had to be ...

'Nathan? Is that you?'

She spun around to confront their captor.

'Fuck!'

He had a gun pointing directly at her.

'We don't have long, ladies, so let's do this quickly. I'm sorry to involve Isobel in this, but you know how it is ... wrong time, wrong place. I expected to find you in the cottage when I finally figured out how to get in. I can't believe you've come straight here, Katy. That's better than I could have hoped for.'

'What the hell is this about?'

'Throw that knife away from you, Katy. What were you expecting to do, peel potatoes?'

He laughed at his own joke.

Katy threw the knife. Nathan had changed a lot since she'd last seen him. He was big, it was the weight of middle age. He had a beard and was well-groomed, not the sort of person who should be wielding a gun.

'Is it you who's been sending the letters, Nathan? How did you know where I was?'

'Jesus, Katy. Shut the fuck up! I wish I'd had a gun last time we were here. You and Emma should come with a mute button. You drove me insane on that holiday.'

'Let me down, Nathan ... please.'

Isobel had found the courage to speak.

'We need to make this fast.'

Nathan moved over to the tea chest and kicked it away.

Izzy's body dropped hard. The noose took her weight and it pulled tight around her neck. She was fighting for her life. Her legs kicked and her hands moved up to the rope, trying desperately to loosen it.

'Sorry, Izzy,' he said, 'but you should have stayed out of this.'

Katy rushed forward. Nathan levelled the gun at her and she stopped dead in her tracks.

'Damn it, Nathan. You can't just leave her there. You piece of shit, let her down!'

'Your turn next,' Nathan sneered. 'We'll wait a moment for Izzy to stop thrashing around, and then I'll need to be on my way.'

The sound of a car driving up the track at speed made Nathan turn to look. Katy took her opportunity. She lunged for a half brick that was beside her on the floor and threw it directly at him. It struck him squarely on his forehead, drawing blood. He pointed his gun and fired at her, but the bullet missed its target. She screamed and ducked into the dining area.

It had to be Buchanan. Isobel's body was still – she'd passed out from lack of oxygen. Nathan seemed to forget about Katy. He walked over to the front window frame and looked out at the new arrival. He smiled to himself. This was fast becoming a reunion. He recognised Buchanan immediately. After the fire he'd spent a lot of time shut up in interview rooms with that bastard. He'd smelled a rat, and wouldn't leave Nathan alone. Fuck him. He was taking a bullet too. In for a penny, in for a pound.

He raised the gun and aimed at Buchanan's head, following him as he neared the bungalow. It was like being at the shooting range, only it was a bit harder to hit a moving target. Stupid bastard, Nathan thought as he squeezed the trigger. Buchanan dropped to the ground. One moment he was walking, the next he was motionless, lying in a growing pool of blood.

Nathan turned to deal with Katy, but she hadn't wasted the opportunity. She'd grabbed an off-cut of wood from the interior wall construction and struck him hard on the head as he turned around to shoot her. He fell to one knee, still holding the gun. Katy struck him again, so hard that it scared her. This time he dropped and didn't get up.

As soon as she saw him go down, she rushed over to Isobel.

'Oh God, Izzy. Please be alive, please don't die.'

She picked up the tea chest and tried to place it under Isobel's legs. It didn't work. She was a dead weight.

Katy rushed to pick up the kitchen knife, which was lying on the floor where she'd thrown it. She climbed up onto the tea chest sawing away at the rope. Nathan was beginning to stir.

'Cut, damn you. Cut!' she shouted, aware of Nathan moving to her side. 'Come on, Izzy. Come on!'

Nathan had got to his feet. She could sense him checking out his head, feeling for damage. That didn't take long. He was scrabbling for his gun.

Stupid cow, she thought. Why didn't I take the bloody gun!

She was cutting furiously now. She knew that she had only seconds left. At last she cut through enough of the rope for the final strands to break and Izzy crashed to the ground, her head striking the side of the tea chest. Katy threw the knife at Nathan. It was a useless gesture, but it startled him enough for his next shot to completely miss her.

Running for her life, Katy jumped through the glassless window frame of the lounge area, and out into the back garden. Where were the police? Surely Buchanan would have alerted them? What about Emma? Cautiously, Katy moved around the side of the building towards the front. She didn't know if Nathan had followed her out the back or if he was about to appear from the front of the building. She got her answer. He was behind her. He shot. The bullet hit her this time, taking a chunk out of her calf.

'Jesus Christ!'

Half-running, half-hobbling, Katy knew that she'd have to make it to the motorcycle if she was going to get away from there. Or had Nathan left the keys in the car? She couldn't chance it. He was angry and he wasn't going to stop until he got her.

As she ran towards the bike, she saw Buchanan's body lifeless on the ground. She gasped at the sight, but there was nothing she could do for him or for Izzy either. She had to run, to stay alive, to get help. Nathan fired again, hitting the bike. Katy was startled by how close it had been.

There was no time for messing around. She jumped onto the bike, pushed it off the stand, and revved the engine. Nathan shot again. Her T-shirt was wet. He'd struck her in the shoulder. Her leg was agony, but she was still moving, she had to keep going. The next shot might kill her. He was a maniac. How many bullets were in that gun?

Different thoughts flashed across her mind. Nathan was almost upon her, pulling up his weapon and aiming it directly at her head. She flicked the gear lever, pulled the throttle and roared forwards. He held up the gun, but realised it was useless. He'd need to go after her in the car.

Katy looked more like a speedway rider than a motorcyclist. She almost tipped the bike as she spun around tightly to head for the track that led back to the road. She put out her foot, wincing with pain as she steadied herself. She revved and drove the bike forwards, away from Nathan. He was in the driver's seat already, not bothering to shut the passenger door. He pulled the car around in the driveway and began his pursuit of Katy along the track.

She was struggling to steady herself. She knew that he was right on her tail, but the track was too uneven for her to risk any great speed. She could hear him rev the engine as he sped towards the rear wheel of the bike. Instinctively, she pulled back the throttle to outrun him, but it was too fast for the track, she couldn't control the bike. She was on a bend now, and as she struggled to hold on she ran straight into a police car which was racing up the track towards the bungalow.

Katy heard the bike crash into the front of the car, and felt the sharp jolt as she tipped forward and began to fly over the bonnet and then the roof. The last thing she felt was the thud of her body smashing onto the ground.

For a moment Katy thought that she was waking up in bed, but then the pain came again. Her leg. Her shoulder. Now her head. God, her head hurt. And her arm. Was it sprained? Broken perhaps. What had happened? She'd been on the bike and she'd had an accident. She was still alive. Nathan ... Where was Nathan? She could hear him shouting. He was some distance away. The cops, had they got him?

Lying still on the ground, she tried to scan the area ahead. Nathan was at the side of the police car still holding the gun. Had he shot the police? Surely he hadn't shot the police. A helicopter was hovering overhead.

'You stupid little bitch, Katy!' he shouted. 'Look at what you've made me do. You always got in the way. It was you who came between me and Elijah. Well, fuck you. This last bullet is for you!'

He was taking his time now. It seemed that he'd given himself up for dead, but he wanted to kill her first. Why? What had she done to him? Katy considered talking to him. Would more police be on the way? That had to be a police helicopter. How quickly could they respond to an armed incident in such a rural area?

Katy looked to the dense forest at her side. It was worth a try. He wouldn't waste his last bullet, not unless he intended to kill her with his bare hands. He was walking over to her. The pain was excruciating. Surely she wouldn't have to run for long. They'd come soon, wouldn't they?

She rolled onto her side, crunching a stone against her ribs. At least that pain was better than being hit by another bullet. She forced herself to her feet. Her leg was wet with blood, but she could do it. She had to do it. She staggered into the trees and ducked to the left. Keep going downhill, she thought. Aim for the road. The loud chopping sound of the helicopter filled the air. They'd never see her in the trees. Had she been foolish heading for cover?

Behind her Nathan was cursing as he crashed through the undergrowth. What had she done to make him so furious ... so furious that he wanted to kill her – and Izzy too? Katy knew that she had to force the fear back down. She couldn't think about Izzy or Buchanan – and whatever he'd done to the police officers in the car. She had to stay alive.

The trees were even closer together. They were pines of some sort, and the low growth was scratching her face. Nathan would have the same to contend with, it would slow him down too. She moved as fast as she could, dragging her injured leg and almost crippled with the pain. It would be easier to give up. It hurt too much, she was so tired. Maybe she'd die anyway, she had to be losing a lot of blood.

Out of nowhere, it seemed, she stumbled into a clearing.

She was trapped. Nathan was right behind her and there was no place to hide. He had her. There was nothing else she could do. She'd done her best. She was out of options.

Nathan was as surprised as Katy to find the clearing.

'Got you, you bloody bitch!' he shouted, striking her face with the side of the gun. She sank to the ground. This was it. She was giving up. That was enough. She had nothing left to fight with. She closed her eyes and waited, the air filled with the persistent whine of that damn helicopter, and then everything went black.

The first face that Katy saw was Emma's.

'At last!' she smiled. 'I've been in a right state here. We thought we'd lost you.'

No grapes and sympathy from Ems then. Katy felt like death warmed up. She could sense that her head was bandaged. Her arm was in a sling too. It didn't hurt anymore, though. They must have given her some decent drugs.

'Do you want some water?' Emma asked.

'My mouth tastes like it's full of sawdust,' Katy replied. She had to force her voice to work. A sip of water helped. She was sitting propped up in the bed. It was a hospital, of course, and now that she was awake the medical staff were alert, wanting to run some routine checks. It seemed to take forever. Katy was desperate to talk to Emma, but at the same time she didn't even want to start. Was Izzy dead? What about Buchanan? Maybe it would be better to go back to sleep and pretend it had never happened.

Finally the nurses left her alone. Emma had sat patiently throughout.

'What day is it?' Katy asked.

'Friday. You've been out for a while. I had to finish school early. Thanks for that. It's a long half-term for me!'

Katy smiled. Her face felt so stiff.

'Have I been pissing and shitting in this bed?'

It seemed a ridiculous thing to ask, but it had suddenly occurred to her.

'Don't ask,' Emma replied. 'Try not to think about it. The nurses see worse every day.'

Katy could feel her face reddening. Somehow she'd survived Nathan's violent assault and here she was worrying about the toilet arrangements.

'Do you want to know what happened?' Emma asked. She couldn't wait to tell. Katy nodded.

'It was a fucking mess, to put it simply. You won't believe it.'

'What about Izzy? Buchanan? They're dead, they must be.'

Emma's face changed. Her expression became sombre.

'You saved Izzy,' she said. 'You're a flipping hero. Her neck looks horrible, it's bruised and bloody, but there was no brain damage. Everyone was really worried about that, but they're as sure as they can be that she's going to be okay.'

'Have you seen her?' Katy asked.

'Yes, briefly. Nancy is here too. She's nice. She knows about what happened between me and Izzy when we were students. I never realised how much it had meant to Izzy. I apologised to her but I still feel really crap about it.'

'What about Buchanan. Is he dead?'

'Life support,' Emma replied. 'They flew him down to a head trauma unit in Glasgow. Poor bugger only had a short time to go until he retired – imagine that happening to him here of all places. He must have spent his life rescuing cats from trees, and then this happens in his final months as a cop. How rubbish is that?'

'Will he make it? Do they know yet?'

'Yes, he'll make it, but he won't be doing any more policing. His wife reckons he'll be pensioned off. It'll take some rehabilitation, so retirement starts for him as of now.'

'You spoke to her?'

'No, we – you – have a Police Liaison Officer. Only, you haven't been awake so they're keeping me up-to-date. They're going to want to talk to you, they're desperate to fill in the gaps.'

'I'm not sure I can even remember,' Katy said. She took another sip of water. She couldn't get her voice going.

'What happened to Nathan?'

'Dead. He was shot by a police marksman, and in the nick of time too. He was about to put a bullet through your head.'

'How the hell did he even have that bloody gun? Nobody has guns in this country unless they're a farmer.'

'Nathan did. Some posh shooting club near Aberdeen. Fully licensed. He's a respectable member of the community, you know. Only, it turns out he's not. He never has been.'

'What do you mean?'

'He's been having gay affairs for years. Quite nasty stuff, a bit violent. Sarah has suspected for ages, but never really knew.'

'Oh God, Sarah. Have you seen her?'

'Yes, she came down here to visit you, but you were out cold. She's in a real mess. She doesn't know whether to feel grief for Nathan or to hate him. She's gone home now. She's not in a good way.'

'This fucking place!' Katy cursed. She'd found her voice again. Swearing had helped to clear her throat. 'It's messed up so many lives. It's so beautiful up here ... but look at the damage that's been done.'

'I know. Sarah said the marriage had always been difficult. She said it's like a part of Nathan was never there. Well, we know what part that was now, the heterosexual part.'

'Buchanan thought there might have been some incident between Elijah and Nathan. Maybe that's what this is all about.'

'I'm not sure if we'll ever know. It's all so long ago. They've gone right back to our university days. They're tracking down Nathan's personal tutor, trying to see if he told them anything at the time. He's been living a secret life for years though. Poor sod, why didn't he just come out?'

Katy thought about that one. Maybe it was easier to keep the lie going than it was to risk revealing everything. She didn't know. Or maybe she did have some insight. She thought of how long she'd stayed with Louis, even when she knew it was wrong. Perhaps that's how Nathan had felt. He had a job, a wife, a professional reputation to uphold. It might have been easier to sustain the pretence than to reveal the truth.

'I feel like I have a million questions to ask,' Katy said. 'I can barely take it all in.'

'I need to apologise to you, Katy. It was all my fault. What happened, it was my fault.'

Katy looked into Emma's face. It was a ridiculous thing to say. How could it possibly be Emma's fault. She'd been in London the whole time.

'How? How can this possibly have anything to do with you? It was Nathan. He's the one to blame.'

'It was through me that he knew what you were doing. I let him install some piece of software on my phone and laptop so he could sort out my technical problems. It was amazing, he could do it from Aberdeen or wherever it was he was working. He did fix them too, but he didn't remove the software. The bastard could help himself to my phone and PC to see exactly what I was doing. The police reckon he was reading all my emails and all our chats, and that's how he knew what you were up to. He's a clever bastard, and I'm a stupid bitch. I'm really sorry.'

'It's not your fault,' Katy consoled her, reaching out to squeeze her hand. 'None of us walks away from this completely free of blame. It all goes back to that blasted holiday.'

***

'I'm going to miss you so much.'

Katy couldn't remember seeing Emma so upset, not even after the fire. Paige gave her a hug. They'd become good friends over the past three months. Solus Na Madainn had been a great place to recover and set her head straight. And now her old friend and her new friend were seeing her off from Inverness Airport. She was heading for Majorca. It was the sunniest place that they flew to from there. All she wanted was to find a nice beach and forget everything.

'You will let me know how you're getting on, won't you?' Paige asked.

'I will. I'm usually terrible at keeping in touch, but I promise I will. I'm really grateful for everything, Paige. What can I say?'

Katy's mobile phone cheeped and she checked the text that had just arrived.

'It's from Buchanan telling me to have a good flight. That was nice of him.'

'It's good to see he's up and about again,' Emma said.

'He emailed me yesterday. He reckons he'll be out of his

wheelchair by the end of the month. I owe him a lot – I hope he understood that when we visited him.'

'I think he got the message,' Emma said. 'It was something to do with the tears and hugs. He definitely picked up your vibe.'

Katy thought over the past few weeks. Sarah had come to see them, but it was all still so raw for her. She had discovered that her entire adult life had been built on a lie. Izzy and Nancy had been over too. The scarring on Izzy's neck was so bad that she would always have to wear a scarf to conceal it. She'd sent the motorbike the same way as the cigarettes and had reinvested the insurance money in a vehicle of the four-wheeled variety. Nancy was lovely. She'd completely changed Izzy from the girl that they'd known when they were teenagers. She seemed happy. It wasn't lost on Katy that if Nathan had had the courage to live his life openly, maybe things would have been different for him too. His hatred for Katy must have festered for years.

'I've got to go,' Katy said. 'I'll miss boarding if I don't go now. I love you both. I'll send you a postcard. Probably. Or probably not. But I love you both anyway.'

Katy picked up her rucksack and walked through the gate. Hand baggage only. Nothing that would be a burden. Onto a new life.

July 1999 It began as an innocent squabble and it ended in a death. They would all live to regret that day. Not one of them would have wanted it to end the way it did. Those tragic events would shape their lives for more years than they could possibly have imagined.

Three of them would know a partial truth about what happened that night. For Nathan, hatred and indignation would eat away at him for years. At last, terrified that the secret of his sexuality might come out, he would be driven to cover his tracks and take his deluded revenge for a love that would never have been reciprocated.

For Izzy, it was the horror of knowing that it was her cigarette that had burned down the lodge. That knowledge never left her, but she would eventually find the love of her life and put it behind her. She knew too that there must have been some other reason why Elijah didn't make it out of the blazing building.

For Katy, those tragic events would create a perpetual restlessness and a burden of guilt that would affect her relationships for her whole life. They'd been so young, but what happened that day would stay with them until they drew their last breath.

Nathan had been in love with Elijah. He had known it for some time and he was sure Elijah reciprocated his feelings. He'd been Elijah's confidant throughout the bullying episodes – they were close, they shared every hope, worry and fear. When Katy came along Nathan was confused. He detested her and more than anything he wanted her out of the way. When Elijah fell head over heels in love with her, he smouldered with resentment.

He fooled himself that Elijah was testing him, making sure that he was worthy. After all, Sarah clearly wanted to be his girlfriend, but he wasn't interested in her, only as a friend. Surely Elijah felt the same about Katy. For Nathan, Elijah was his first true love and his heart ached with a deep passion for him.

The day that Elijah and Katy fell out, he'd finally resolved to reveal his feelings. They'd been close again that day, the way it had been before Katy came along. He felt invigorated, he was ready to take a chance with Elijah. Katy had been furious with her boyfriend. What to her was outrage at Elijah's insensitivity was to Nathan the inevitable outcome of a doomed relationship. Elijah just hadn't realised it yet.

They were in the bedroom, chatting and laughing. They'd got a few beers down them. Elijah was wheezing a bit – sometimes alcohol made him do that. Asthma could be a nuisance, but he had it under control. Brown puffer, blue puffer, they followed him around everywhere. Only he'd left them in Katy's bag from their day trip.

They were sitting next to each other chatting about the things they'd got up to before Katy arrived on the scene. For Elijah, it was a bit of male bonding, a postponement of the inevitable showdown with his girlfriend. For Nathan, it was something different. For a moment, only a fleeting moment, their faces were close – uncomfortably so for Elijah. But before he had a chance to reposition himself, Nathan moved forward and kissed him on the lips.

Elijah recoiled.

'What the hell was that?'

'I thought ... I thought ...'

Nathan's face was bright red, he'd completely misjudged the situation. He knew it the minute his lips touched Elijah's.

'Damn it, Nathan. What were you even thinking? You know I love Katy, I've told you a million times. Why did you even do that?'

Elijah's wheezing was becoming louder from the stress of what had happened. Nathan felt humiliated, hurt, angry – he was such an idiot. What had he been thinking of?

'I thought ... I thought we were more than friends.'

'No! We're just friends. We were friends. I don't know what say. I don't mind if you're gay, but come on! You've got eyes, you can see how I am about Katy.'

Tears began to drop from Nathan's eyes. This was the first time he'd dared to declare that he might love a man. He was despised by Elijah, he felt sordid and dirty, as if he was some kind of abomination.

'I love you ... I only wanted to tell you that I love you.'

'Leave me,' said Elijah. 'Give me some space to think this through.'

'Please don't tell the others,' Nathan begged. 'Please don't tell.'

'Just go!' Elijah shouted. He was wheezing badly now, he needed a moment to calm down and regulate his breathing.

'Are you okay?' Nathan asked, turning back at the door.

'Can you ask Katy if she's got my puffers? I think they're in her bag.'

Nathan nodded, trying his best to conceal his tears. He'd have to keep his voice steady and find somewhere to go until the redness had gone from his eyes.

'Elijah says can you let him have his puffers,' he managed to blurt out in as steady a voice as he could muster, before rushing out of the front door to get some privacy.

'Fuck him!' Katy said. 'Let him get them himself if he needs them. He knows where they are.'

At the moment she said that, Elijah collapsed on the Z-bed from lack of oxygen. It was a long time since he'd had such a bad attack, but the stress had been building all afternoon. He'd been trying to manage it, breathing deeply and methodically. There was no way he'd been prepared to ask Katy for the puffers that were in her bag. He was determined to do without them until she came to apologise. He was now regretting that choice.

As Elijah lay slowly suffocating on the bed, Isobel's cigarette stub came flying through the open window. It wasn't intentional, just a careless act. It was only when the investigation was complete that she'd discover what she'd done. After all, she was the only one who smoked at the time. It would be a habit that Nathan took up shortly after Elijah's death.

And so the tragedy played out. As the cigarette began to burn the rug beneath the windowsill, Elijah struggled for breath, wondering where Katy was with his puffers. He couldn't cry out, and by the time the smoke had filled his room and a spark turned to searing flames, he was unconscious.

It was only when the friends had come together at the front of the house that Katy asked where Elijah was. They'd assumed he'd jumped out of the window and run around the back of the building – why wouldn't he when the cries of 'Fire!' went up? But Elijah was dead by then. And as they stood watching the flames destroy the lodge, nobody would ever know that it was really Katy who had killed Elijah, for hers was the final kindness that might have saved him.

Find out more about Paul J. Teague's thrillers at https://paulteague.co.uk/

23198423R00098

Printed in Poland
by Amazon Fulfillment
Poland Sp. z o.o., Wrocław